LARRY

THE
KING OF
ROCK
AND
ROLL

LARRY

THE KING OF ROCK AND ROLL

A NOVEL BY

IRIS RAINER DART AND
JOYCE BROTMAN

G. P. PUTNAM'S SONS

G. P. PUTNAM'S SONS
A division of Penguin Young Readers Group.
Published by The Penguin Group.
Penguin Group (USA) Inc., 375 Hudson Street, New York, NY 10014, U.S.A.
Penguin Group (Canada), 90 Eglinton Avenue East, Suite 700, Toronto, Ontario, Canada
M4P 2Y3 (a division of Pearson Penguin Canada Inc.).
Penguin Books Ltd, 80 Strand, London WC2R 0RL, England.
Penguin Ireland, 25 St. Stephen's Green, Dublin 2, Ireland (a division of Penguin Books Ltd.).
Penguin Group (Australia), 250 Camberwell Road, Camberwell, Victoria 3124, Australia
(a division of Pearson Australia Group Pty Ltd).
Penguin Books India Pvt Ltd, 11 Community Centre, Panchsheel Park,
New Delhi—110 017, India.
Penguin Group (NZ), Cnr Airborne and Rosedale Roads, Albany, Auckland 1310,
New Zealand (a division of Pearson New Zealand Ltd).
Penguin Books (South Africa) (Pty) Ltd, 24 Sturdee Avenue, Rosebank,
Johannesburg 2196, South Africa.
Penguin Books Ltd, Registered Offices: 80 Strand, London WC2R 0RL, England.

Design by Katrina Damkoehler. Text set in Stone Sans and Moorbacka.

Library of Congress Cataloging-in-Publication Data
Dart, Iris Rainer.
Larry, the king of rock and roll / by Iris Rainer Dart and Joyce Brotman.   p. cm.
Summary: Not only can Larry the dog talk, he can also sing, but when these
unusual talents come to the attention of his family, the public, and dogdom,
Larry is faced with problems he never imagined.
[1. Dogs-Fiction. 2. Pets-Fiction. 3. Fathers-Fiction.] I. Brotman, Joyce. II. Title.
PZ7.D2543La 2007   [Fic]-dc22   2005032667

ISBN 978-0-399-24546-6
1 3 5 7 9 10 8 6 4 2
First Impression

THANKS TO:

Elaine Markson
Gary Johnson
John Rudolph
Dr. Rob Fisher
Brad Freeman

And all the Maltese in our lives:
Lily, Daisy, Fluffy, Mimi, Casper,
Ruby, Max, Roxy, Lola
and the late great Guido,
who started it all.

This book and everything I write
is dedicated to Steve, Greg, Rachel, Lydia,
Jonathan, Maya and Stuey—I.R.D.

In Memory of my parents.
For Peter Heft and, of course, for Maggie—J.B.

1
Larry

Okay! Okay! I'm sorry. I know you think I owe you an explanation for what I did, and you're right. It was terrible. I was awful, but please . . . please . . . please let me tell you what happened and then I hope you can find it in your hearts to forgive me.

I guess it all started with Courtney Mason. I'm sure you've seen her on MTV or in concert or maybe you have her CDs. She's on the cover of every magazine there is, with headlines about all the crazy things she's done. So I guess it was no surprise when all of a sudden she threw a hissy fit right in the studio just as she was about to record the last song for her new CD. She was mad as a snake! Knocking down music stands and using language that wasn't very nice.

Tom looked over at me and saw me covering my ears so

I wouldn't hear some of those words she was saying. And, after freaking out big-time, Courtney stormed out of the studio. "I'm never coming back!" she screamed.

The whole band was blown away. Nobody moved for at least a minute. Courtney's manager—who never takes off his dark glasses—seemed to be super-embarrassed by the way Courtney acted and got real apologetic. He said, "Oh, please don't hate her. After all, it was just that one little song she didn't like. Once we find a better song, Courtney will be right back here to finish making the CD. And," he added, "you'll all come back too and help her make it a big hit. Right?"

I looked over at Tom and he looked at me and we shrugged and packed up. We were both bummed. Especially Tom. He and his wife, Peggy, divorced a few months ago. She lives only a few blocks away and they share custody of their awesome ten-year-old daughter, Cathy, but losing their family still made Tom sad and Cathy super-sad. I was sad for them too. But Cathy hardly ever complained when she had to move back and forth every week between her mom's and dad's houses.

"Hey, Tommy," Artie called out as we were leaving. Artie's our buddy who plays lead guitar. "Maybe you ought to send Courtney that new song of yours!"

"Yeah, sure. If I could ever finish the darned thing," Tom mumbled. I heard him sigh under his breath. "But I probably never will."

Now, I always like to think of myself as tough, but hearing him say that made me want to cry. Being Tom's best friend, I always tried to make him laugh when he was feeling low. But that afternoon I couldn't even get him to crack a smile.

Tom pulled his truck out of the studio parking lot and I settled into my seat thinking it was going to be a long night of feeling bad. But as we pulled up at the house, there was Peggy waiting to drop Cathy off for the weekend. When Tom saw Cathy, his face lit up, as always.

"Daddy . . . Larry!" Cathy hollered happily, running to meet us. "See ya, Mom!" Peggy waved good-bye to us as she drove off. Tom whirled Cathy around with a big hug and then he went inside while Cathy and I stayed outside to play Frisbee.

"Okay, Larry," she called just before the Frisbee sailed through the air. "Back up for a long one."

We could hear Tom tinkling away on his old upright piano. Tom's real job was to play the piano for singers when they recorded their songs but, at home when he was alone, he wrote his own songs. Now he was noodling on that song

Artie had been bugging him about. He'd play a few bars . . . then sing some of the lyrics . . . then sigh a big sigh . . . and then start again. But it didn't sound as if he was getting very far.

He'd been stuck for a long time on the part of the song they call the "bridge." The bridge is that middle part of a song that has a different tune than the rest of it. No matter how hard he tried, poor Tom just couldn't come up with a bridge that worked for that song. And it was too bad because the rest of the song was very cool.

Soon it was time for Tom to cook dinner, so he stopped to make some hamburgers, humming the song while he cooked. Later that night I heard him in the bathroom, brushing his teeth and humming the song while he brushed, humming it some more as he climbed into bed, and humming it even more as he drifted off to sleep. But he couldn't finish it and my heart broke for him.

Okay, this is the part where I guess I made a humongous mistake and should have stayed out of it. But I swear I wasn't doing it for myself. I was only doing it because I was Tom's best friend and he needed my help.

When I saw that Tom and Cathy were both sound asleep, I crept into the music room where Tom had been writing the song on the computer with this special software he has just for songwriting, and I typed in the words and music for the bridge he hadn't been able to finish. But I really was doing it for Tom. I was thinking "The Elves and the Shoemaker." You know that story? Where the elves make the shoes and the shoemaker gets the credit?

When I finished I sang the song softly to myself and nodded happily. I knew I'd done a great job! "Larry," I said to myself, "you're a heck of a good friend." Then I went back to the family room, plopped on the couch and curled up with a smile.

It was the sound of the piano that woke me the next morning. Tom was in the music room playing the song.

"Jeez," I heard him say as he played the bridge, "I must have been super-tired last night. I don't even remember finishing the song. But here it is."

"You finished it?" Cathy asked, running in. "Wow, Dad, play it for me!"

I was trying to be cool, so I didn't move from the couch or make a sound while Tom played the song from the top. It was a very catchy tune; he played it great and I got excited waiting for him to get to my part. At last he pounded out the bridge and sang my smart, funny lyrics.

Then he stopped and burst out laughing. "Jeez! I don't believe I wrote that," he said.

Yeah, well, no duh, I thought. But I just played dumb, if you know what I mean. And you won't believe what he said next.

"I must have been out-of-my-mind tired last night. This bridge really stinks big-time!"

I could feel my face getting hot the way it does when I'm angry. Now when I look back I think I probably should have counted to ten, or whatever people do to stop themselves from blurting out their hurt feelings, but I didn't. Instead I rushed into that room, looked at Tom and screamed, "On your best day you couldn't write something that good! *I* wrote it!"

Oops.

I knew as soon as I saw the expressions on both Tom's and Cathy's faces that they were completely weirded out to know I was the one who finished the song. And even worse, they were stunned that I was mouthing off like the hothead that I am.

Then they both said at the same time, "Larry, you talked!"

I guess they were so astonished because what I haven't mentioned before is . . . I'm their dog.

2
Cathy

Help! I can't believe it. My dog can speak! And I don't mean the way other people hold a treat above their dog's head and say, "Speak!" and then the dog barks so he'll get the treat. I mean he can say real words.

Larry is a Maltese. A cute little white furry thing my best friend Lily says looks like a bedroom slipper that barks or a throw pillow with eyes—or what Derek, a boy I don't like, calls a dropkick dog. I know that's pretty awful. I wanted to scream at creepy Derek when he said that, but I didn't because I've been called into the school counselor's office already for crying in class a few times. And I knew if I screamed at Derek I'd get called in there again.

Mostly I cry when I think about my parents getting a

divorce. I still don't understand that! I mean, they got along. When Lily's parents got a divorce, she said they fought all the time. But my mom and dad like each other a lot. I can tell. They're nice to each other. They like to do all the same things. They both love the LA Lakers and they both go to the games. They just don't go together anymore. So I don't understand it. And now our family is getting even more confusing. Because my dog just talked to me.

"You can talk?" Dad kept asking over and over. "You can talk? You've been our dog for seven years, and now you're telling us this? Why didn't you ever talk before?"

"Because you never insulted my talent before!" Larry answered.

And then I saw Artie's car pull up outside and I panicked. "Dad, Larry, shush! If anybody finds out about this, we're in trouble!" Both Dad and Larry stopped talking and looked at me. "You've seen those movies! *King Kong, E.T. . . . Dumbo*? Remember how the scientists and the circus people all wanted to turn them into freaks? If anybody else finds out our dog can talk, they'll want to take him away from us, and then he'll belong to the scientists."

Well, I guess that scared them because as soon as

Artie opened the door, all three of us tried to act as if nothing had happened.

"Yo!" Artie said, giving me a hug. "What's up?" He looked from me to Dad to Larry. "Hey, pooch!" he said as he got down to ruffle Larry's fur.

"I been thinkin' about that song of yours," Artie said to Dad, who still had the glazed look in his eyes of a man who'd just heard his dog holler at him. "You have to finish it, pal. It really is right for Courtney. I know we all think she's a royal pain. But who cares? Let her be a pain as long as she records your song, right?"

"I finished the song," Dad said, but when Larry made a sound that sounded halfway between a bark and a cough, Dad realized he'd said that wrong. "What I mean to say is the song's finished," Dad added.

"No joke?" Artie said. "So what are you waitin' for? Play it for me."

Dad started to protest. "Aw, not yet. I still have to . . ."

But Artie stopped him and nudged him over to the piano bench and said, "Hey, this is me. Your pal. Remember? Play the darned thing, will ya? I want to hear it."

Larry scooted up next to me and we stood side by side as Dad played the new version of the song for Artie, who smiled a big smile while he listened. And when Dad got to the bridge, Artie closed his eyes, kind of swaying back and forth and nodding.

As soon as Dad hit the last note Artie jumped up and down, hollering, "Awesome, awesome! Best thing you ever wrote. And that new bridge is phenomenal!" He grabbed Dad and hugged him as Larry—and I couldn't believe he did this—shouted out, "Ha!!!" When Artie looked around to see who said that, I quickly added, "Chooo!" I hoped it sounded like I'd sneezed and not that my dog was yelling out in triumph.

"Tomorrow," Artie said, "you're making me a tape of this song. If Courtney doesn't want it—and frankly I think it's too good for her—we'll find someone who does."

Whenever I stay at my dad's, Mom calls me every night to ask me how my day was and to say good night. Tonight, when she called, she said, "Hi, Pumpkin, what's new?"

"Nothing much," I answered. But it was a little white lie. A little furry white lie.

3
Larry

In my whole life I'd never been invited to a pajama party. Cathy and her girlfriends were always having them and I'd watch with envy. They'd pile onto her bed and stay up until all hours of the night giggling and talking. I'd listen to them asking each other a million questions and telling each other their deepest, darkest secrets.

Now that she found out I could talk, Cathy wanted to have a pajama party with just me! And tonight she wanted me to tell her *my* deepest darkest secrets. So I did. I let loose with stuff I'd wanted to say for years.

"I guess the first secret is: You always thought you chose me," I told her. "But the truth is I chose you."

Cathy let out a giggle. "That's not true," she said. "Even though I was only three, I can still remember that day."

"I remember the details, though. Because dogs never for-get," I said.

"No. That's elephants," she said, and we both laughed.

"You were running up and down at the shelter, asking, 'What do you think, Daddy? Which dog should we take home?' You kept looking around at all the dogs who were lying there paying no attention to you. So I whimpered and followed you up and down the run, panting and putting my paws up on the fence, cocking my head to the side to get your attention in a pose I knew made me look especially cute. And then you stopped and said, 'He likes me!' and I nodded as if to say yes. And you squealed, 'I want *that* one, Daddy!' and you pointed to me. I remember how my heart was pounding with excitement."

Cathy laughed. "I'm so glad you convinced me to pick you." She hugged me with a big warm Cathy hug. "Even before you started talking to us, I always thought I knew what you were trying to say," Cathy said. "I mean, when I take you to the groomer and you get all trembly and sad. I can tell you don't like her."

"Well, you wouldn't like her either," I said. "My bath-water's always freezing. And, as if that's not bad enough, she scrubs me too hard and she uses that noisy blow-dryer on my fur. Then she puts a stupid bow on my collar and makes me look like a wuss. So now that I can speak my mind, can we please change groomers? And tell the new one: No more dopey bows. I'm a guy!"

"Larry, I'm so sorry. I thought you liked the way you looked. I mean, I know having a shampoo is no fun, but you looked so great afterward and you always strutted around the house as if you knew it. I've even seen you check yourself out in the mirror, and I swear I've seen you smile." Then Cathy ruffled my fur. "But isn't it great that *now* you can tell me everything you think? What you like. What you don't like."

"Ha," I said. "You wanna hear all my pet peeves?" Then I thought about it. "Pet peeves from a peeved pet. That's funny." We both laughed out loud at that.

Being able to be myself with her at last felt so good. There were so many times over the years I'd wanted to laugh out loud but was afraid I'd give myself away. Now life was going to be beautiful.

"You won't have to do anything you don't want to do anymore," Cathy said, stroking my fur. "Well, you may have to do it, but at least now you'll be able to complain about it."

Then she patted my head, and whenever she does that I fall apart. Sometimes I think my whole life is lived just for those nice little pats she likes to give me. Scratches behind the ear aren't bad either.

"Do you know how hard it's been for me not to let you know I can talk? Like the other day when you came home from school feeling sad because you thought Peter, that boy in your class who you think is so cute, doesn't pay attention to you? Well, I wanted to tell you that when we were at the park and I was resting under the tree watching you play soccer with your friends, I heard Peter tell his friend John that he thought you were really cool. I wanted to tell you he said that to make you feel better. But I had to keep pretending that I couldn't say a word. Just the way I've been doing for years."

"Really? Peter thought I was cool? What else, my sweet little poochie?" she asked. "Tell me more."

"Well, there is the matter of that stupid leash," I said. I mean, what the heck? How many times was a guy like me gonna have a chance to get all this off my chest?

"Your nice leash?" she said, surprised.

"How would you like to be walking down the street tied to someone else? It's embarrassing."

"But we were always afraid you'd run away."

"Get real," I said. "Why would I leave? I get regular meals, fresh water and a walk from time to time. I'm not going any-where. So I don't need to wear a leash.

"And why," I went on, feeling very sure of myself, "if I may be so bold as to ask, do I sit *under* the table? You say I'm a member of this family and yet all the rest of you get to sit in chairs. The only good thing about being down there is that when Artie comes over, he's such a slob he drops half his dinner on the floor."

"Not sure I can get Dad to let you sit at the table," Cathy said seriously.

"He'll get used to it," I told her. "Didn't we train him to let me sleep on your bed? Didn't we train him to take me out when I tap him on the leg with my paw? He was going to leave me at home all day while he went to work. I made such a scene every night when he got home, yelping and running in circles, that he finally figured out it was easier just to take me with him. So you see? He's not so dumb. He can learn new tricks."

"He never takes *me* to work with him," Cathy said.

"Believe me, you're lucky," I told her. "You don't have to see the kinds of scenes like the one I saw with Courtney Mason. What a wacko!"

We talked all night, about so many things. "I love that

you taught me to catch a Frisbee," I said. "There was a while when I was sure I was the only dog on the planet that kept missing them. And I love the long walks we take together. And how cozy I feel when I curl up at your feet when you do your homework." I took a deep breath. "Those are my favorite things so far."

"My favorite thing was the day last month when I was sick with the flu," Cathy said. "You jumped up on the bed and never left all day. And what about the time Christina told everyone at school I had a crush on Peter? I was so sad I came home and hid under the bed."

"I remember," I told her.

"You crawled under there too and snuggled up next to me for hours, licking my arm until I felt better. Larry, I'd do anything for you," she said. "Tell me what I can do to make sure you're happy."

"You mean it?" I asked.

"Anything," Cathy said.

"How about getting me my own computer?" I tried.

"Larry, what would you do with a computer?"

"I've already written a song. Who knows what I can do next?" I said. And then I winked and she laughed.

4
Cathy

The next morning, we started operating under Larry's rules and I must admit it was kind of fun, like when I used to play "tea party" with Lily.

Larry sat down at the table and had me tie a napkin around his neck. "I'm having Cheerios," I said to Larry. "What about you?"

"Let's see . . ." He thought about it for a minute. "How about bacon and sausage and ham?"

"Gee, that's a very big order." My dad laughed as he walked into the room.

"Yeah, well, I'm finally getting to choose my own food and I'm starting out in style," Larry said. "No more of this dog food for me. Have you ever tasted that kibble?"

Both Dad and I shook our heads no.

"You try a bowl of it. See how you like it," Larry said.

Just then the phone rang. It was Artie calling with big news.

"You played my song for Clementine Flowers without even telling me?" Dad shouted into the phone. Dad was a big fan of Clementine Flowers. We had lots of her CDs and he played them all the time. And Clementine was an even bigger star than Courtney Mason. "In her act? She's going to put it in her act? Whee-o-o-o-o!" He put down the phone and did a happy dance all around the room, singing the song.

"Ham, bacon and sausage. You got it!" Dad sang as he danced out the door to go to the market.

I looked out the window and saw him do a pirouette just before he got into the truck.

"And maybe you should throw in a little T-bone steak for dinner to celebrate," Larry called out.

"While we're waiting for Dad to come back," I said, "let's go to the park!"

"The park it is!" Larry said.

It's funny but once we got to the park, I couldn't stop watching Larry. When he ran and played with the other dogs, I noticed the way he greeted them as they approached him. Not just sniffing and testing each other out the way dogs do but making moves that meant "whaddaya think of my new haircut?" or "wanna hang out with me?" without actually saying the words.

One dog in particular wanted to be Larry's friend. He was a scruffy little Cocker Spaniel whose owner kept shouting to him, "Yo, Fred, c'mere, Fred," but Fred ignored his owner because he only wanted to trail behind Larry.

When I threw the Frisbee to Larry, Fred ran after it too. Larry was getting much better at Frisbee, so he didn't pay much attention when Fred raced across the grassy field faster on his longer legs with an expression on his face that seemed to say, "I got it . . . I got it!" But Larry was fast and he kept slipping around poor Fred just quick enough to jump up and catch the Frisbee in his waiting teeth.

When Larry ran back to me with the Frisbee, the sides of his little mouth were turned up in a smile. He didn't even notice a pretty Maltese watching him from across the park. She was as white as snow and she had one of those fancy doggie haircuts where her long hair trailed almost to the ground. She had the cutest little yellow bows around the topknots. It was kind of the way Mom used to do my hair when I was four.

The Maltese's owner called out to her, "Maggie! Maggie!" but she wasn't listening. She was concentrating on getting Larry's attention. She slowly walked across the grass, pretending not to see him, although she couldn't help but glance over at him every few feet.

It made me giggle to see a girl dog behave that way with a boy dog. And, just like real boys, Larry was too busy running with his buddy Fred to notice her.

By the time Larry and I walked home from the park, we'd made plans to spend the whole weekend together, just hanging out and sharing all the stories we never imagined we'd be able to tell each other. And, of course, Larry talked about how he was looking forward to his T-bone steak.

5
Larry

By now I had been talking for a whole week, and I loved it. It was a lot easier to get what I wanted when I could ask for it. For example: Driving in the car is one of my favorite things to do. It got even better once I made a few adjustments.

"C'mon, Tom. It's not easy to go through life being so tiny. It's a pretty strange view from all the way down here."

"I brought all those living room pillows out to the car just the way you wanted," Tom said. "What is it now?"

"Push them closer to the window," I pressed. Then I looked over at Tom's unhappy face and knew I'd left out the one key word in order to get him to do it. "Please," I said in the most appreciative voice I could muster.

Tom shrugged and pushed the pillows closer to the car window. I jumped on top, testing the height. "Just one more will be perfect," I said, forcing him to go back into the house again.

But I knew it was all worth it when I finally got everything positioned just right. Because that's when Tom opened the back window and I propped my chin so it rested perfectly across the sill. When we pulled out of the driveway, the breeze blew against my face and my ears.

"Aaah . . . This is the best feeling in the world," I sighed. And then I caught sight of myself in the side mirror. I must admit I looked very handsome, like an eagle in flight.

The next day when Tom and I were driving to pick up Cathy at school, I asked him to change the radio station in the car. I asked nicely. Just the way I always do. But Tom was super-annoyed. "I heard you, Larry. I heard you," he said.

He scanned through the channels but we couldn't agree on a station. "What's wrong with this one?" Tom asked when he stopped at the fifth station.

"Elevator music," I muttered. "Not that I've been in that many elevators. But it's boring."

Tom sighed and picked a station. "This one is where we're staying," he said. "You know, Larry, ever since you started to talk, you've been barking out orders . . ." He turned to me with a little smile. "Pardon the expression. And you have an opinion about everything. Well, I'm not so sure I want to hear it."

"Well, maybe you'd want to if you weren't listening to that stupid radio station where the DJ plays the worst music I've ever heard."

"Oh, I get it. You wrote one bridge for one song and now you're an expert all of a sudden," he said.

"Well, I guess I must know *something,* since it was my bridge that got your song sold," I said, getting annoyed too.

I knew I got him with that one because his face flushed red. I guess I shouldn't have done it, but I kept pushing him.

"If I hadn't felt sorry for poor pitiful you, that song would still be sitting in your drawer. But watching you mope around like that was too much for a guy with a heart as big and generous as mine. So I just had to help. If I hadn't finished that song, you'd still be nowhere."

"Don't rub it in, Larry. Just because you did one thing for me doesn't give you the right to run everything. You still live in my house, go for rides in my car, and I don't want—" But before he could finish his sentence, Cathy opened the car door and bounced in with a big smile.

"Hi," she squealed, happy to see us. Then she saw the looks on our faces. "What's the matter? What's going on?"

"All I asked him to do was change the station. I was tired of hearing those same old songs that DJ plays," I said, coldly.

"That's because he thinks he's now Larry, the King of Rock and Roll," Tom said, angrily.

"Stop it, you two!" Cathy said, just as I detected a familiar sound.

"Turn up that radio!" I hollered from the backseat.

"See what I mean! That's exactly what I'm talking about," Tom said. "He shouts orders all day long."

"Turn it up and listen." And that's when we heard what was playing. Our song. The one we wrote. And Clementine Flowers was singing it.

"Oh, wow!" Cathy shrieked. "It's real. It's actually on the radio."

Cathy started slapping high fives with Tom and with me. Even Tom laughed and sang along with the radio.

"Well," Tom said when the song was over, "this calls for a celebration."

"Ice cream!" Cathy shouted.

"Gee, it might spoil your dinner," Tom said, looking at his watch. "Oh, what the heck. We shouldn't have any rules today. Ice cream it is."

But when we pulled up at the ice cream store, Cathy's smile disappeared. She turned to me. "I'm sorry, Larry. I forgot they won't let dogs in." She must have seen the disappointment on my face, because she said, "I'll stay in the car with you, and Dad can bring us the ice cream."

I knew she was only being polite. It was up to me to do the right thing. But I didn't want to.

There was a long silence. Nobody moved. Everyone was waiting for the other person to be generous.

"You two go in. I'll wait here," I finally heard myself say. "But I want *two* scoops of vanilla."

And as I watched Tom and Cathy walk into the ice cream store, I felt very much alone. I knew I was a part of this family. But there were times—and I know they didn't mean it—when it felt like I was only the family dog.

6
Cathy

We walked into the house still licking our ice cream cones. I was happy the celebration made Dad and Larry forget what they were fighting about. And speaking of Larry, he was lucky he was the same color as the vanilla ice cream because he got it all over his muzzle.

I heard the telephone ringing, and grabbed it. "Hi, honey." It was my mom. "Please tell your dad I just heard his song on the radio. The one you sang for me. Tell him I'm very proud of him!"

"Isn't he the greatest?" I asked, hoping a little bit that hearing the song would make her like my dad again the way she used to.

But she only said, "I always knew he was talented."

Then she went on, "Honey, do you think you could stay at your dad's this weekend instead of coming to be with me?"

"Um, sure, I guess," I said, wondering what was up. She never asked me to do that before.

"Richard has to go to Santa Barbara on business and I thought I'd go along for the ride," she explained.

Richard is her boyfriend. I still can't understand why she likes him better than Dad. He isn't nearly as funny. Or as cute. Or as smart. And definitely not as talented.

"Sure, Mom." I forced myself to sound cheerful. "I'll ask Dad if Larry and I can stay here." I hung up the phone, but before I got to ask, I saw Dad sitting at the piano, trying out a new song. He hadn't written a song since Mom moved out, except for that night with Larry. And this one sounded pretty good to me. So good that I couldn't stop myself from humming along as he played it over and over.

But this time when Dad got to the last line, Larry sang out a line that fit the music perfectly. It was just what the song needed. Even Dad whooped his approval when he heard it.

"Larry, that's awesome!" he said. Then he started playing the song like he was a rock star. Standing up at the piano and singing out to the fantasy audience. Larry jumped up on the piano bench. Dad pounded away on the piano while the three of us wailed away.

We were all harmonizing so loudly that we didn't hear the car pull up outside. Or the first few knocks on the door. It was only when Artie really started banging that we realized someone was out there. Dad stopped playing right away. I picked Larry up and carried him to his bed so he could pretend to be an ordinary dog.

"Hey," Larry snapped. "What do you think you're doing?"

"Somebody's here," I whispered.

Larry shook himself out, rearranging his fur the way he liked it. "I could have walked," he grumbled.

Before I could apologize, Artie rushed into the room. "I just heard from my friend who plays drums for Clementine Flowers. Your song is moving up the charts! She's going to sing it in her show on Saturday night at the Hollywood Bowl. I got tickets for all of us!"

Artie slapped Dad on the back and Dad gave him a

little pretend punch on the shoulder. Neither of them was paying attention to Larry or to me. Larry looked like he wasn't happy about being ignored. So I leaned over and scooped him up in my arms and pretended to be dancing around with him. Larry stiffened up and put his head on my shoulder.

"Put me down before I scream," he whispered in my ear.

I laughed out loud. "You wouldn't do that, would you, Larry?"

"Try me." He sounded pretty serious, so I put him down.

By that time Dad and Artie had stopped their celebration. Artie caught his breath and said, "So, big-time songwriter! What else have you got? I heard something pretty great when I was coming up the front walk. Sounded like you had a party going on."

"No party," Dad said. "Just me noodling on a new song."

"You must be some hot noodler," Artie said. "Sounded more like three-part harmony to me."

Dad looked at me and I looked at Larry and Larry just closed his eyes as if he were taking a nap.

"There are only two of us here."

Artie laughed. "Maybe I'm goin' crazy . . ."

"Could be," Dad said. "Lately I think we're all going a little nuts." Then Dad smiled at me and Larry. But Larry just kept his eyes closed, pretending to be asleep.

7
Larry

It was our big night. Clementine Flowers was going to sing our song live onstage at the Hollywood Bowl. From what I've heard, it's a giant outdoor amphitheater where people sit under the stars and hear great music; sometimes by Bach or Brahms, but this time it was going to be a song by Tom and Larry.

Everyone at our house rushed around getting ready to go to the show. Tom was in the shower singing our song at the top of his lungs. He didn't sound half bad, but I wondered if I should take it personally that every time he got to the bridge—the part *I* wrote—he forgot the words.

Cathy was trying on outfits, looking for just the right thing to wear.

"Is this cute?" she asked, holding up a pleated skirt and a flowered blouse.

"Yeah, cute," I answered, barely glancing at her outfit.

"Or should I just wear jeans and a sweater?"

"I'm not really good at fashion." I shrugged. "I always wear the same thing."

Cathy laughed and went off to change her clothes again.

A few minutes later she came into the laundry room. She found me digging in a box, going through all the stupid little doggy outfits they made me wear before I could tell them how dopey I felt in those clothes. Then I found what I was looking for! My fancy red leather collar with little gold hearts. Cathy's mom brought it back from a trip to Paris, but Tom put it away so I wouldn't ruin it.

Tom came in wrapped in a towel, shaving cream all over his face.

"What's all the noise about?" he asked. I guess I must have been making a racket. I looked up at him and didn't answer.

"What's going on here, pooch?" he asked.

"I guess I have to get ready by myself," I said, trying not to sound as hurt as I was feeling. "You're all getting all spiffed up. Surely you don't expect me to go wearing this same old everyday collar, do you?"

"Go?" Tom asked, as if the idea never occurred to him.

I wanted to bite his ankle. "Yeah. *Go!*" I said with all the authority I could muster. "Please be assured I have no intention of missing this. It's my song too, Tom."

"Hey, if it were up to me you'd be there. But . . ."

I cut him off. I knew what he was going to say: *Dogs aren't allowed.* Well, tonight I wasn't buying it! "There's always a way," I told him. "Some dogs are allowed to go everywhere. I see them on TV all the time with their owners carrying them in their arms as if they were little princes."

"I hope you don't expect me to tote you around like that!" Tom snickered at me.

"Of course not. I'm perfectly capable of walking on my own four feet. But I think if you—"

He cut me off right in the middle of my sentence. "Larry, the answer is no!"

That really made me angry. "If I have to call a taxi, I'm going! I'm not going to stay here eating kibble while you two are backstage munching caviar."

"I doubt if they'll have caviar, but tell you what. If they do have it, I'll bring some back for you."

"Ha!" I snorted. "A doggie bag. The biggest insult of all." And with that I stormed out of the room.

I was pouting in my bed in the corner when Cathy came over carrying her backpack. "Now don't throw a fit, Larry, this is the only way it will work." She held the backpack ·

open and told me to climb in. "You're going to have to stay very quiet and pretend to be a toy until we get backstage. Uncle Artie thinks he can handle it from there."

I tried to be insulted, but the truth is I knew it was the only way.

"Okay . . . But only if you put some treats in with me so I'll have something to take my mind off the fact that I'm pretending to be a stuffed animal!" I said. Cathy nodded and we were on our way.

8
Cathy

I held my breath when we got to the entrance to the Hollywood Bowl and Dad handed the usher our tickets. I could feel Larry shift around in my backpack and I was nervous that he would suddenly start yakking and give away our secret.

But he must have found a comfortable spot because after a while he stopped moving. I could hear his little snore coming from inside the bag. I worried that he wouldn't stay asleep for long as we squeezed through the big noisy crowd pouring into the Bowl. The audience was heading to their seats under the star-filled night sky. I always got excited when we went there for concerts, but tonight was super-exciting.

Dad and I showed the usher our backstage passes and he led us through the crowd. I couldn't believe we were going to pull this off. We were actually going to sneak Larry into the Hollywood Bowl without anyone finding out.

Artie was already backstage and he took us into the Green Room . . . which wasn't green but everyone called it that anyway. It's where the performers waited to go onstage and where all their friends waited with them.

But tonight we were the only people there. As I passed the table that was covered with platters of food for the guests, I could feel Larry squirming in the backpack. I think it was the smell of the cheese. Larry loved cheese, so I guessed it was his way of telling me to sneak some into his hiding place.

Before I could figure out how to do that, the concert promoter came running into the Green Room in a panic. "Clementine and her band are late. Their plane is stuck in Phoenix. They'll be here in half an hour, but the audience will have walked out by then. Somebody has to go out there and sing for a while. Just to keep them occupied. Can you do it, Tom?"

"Me? No way!" Dad shouted. "I'm not a performer. I'm just the guy who sits at home in my pajamas and writes songs."

"There's no one else," the promoter said. "And you

have the hottest song on the charts. Just go out and sing it. Tell a little story. By then Clementine will be here and you'll be a big hero."

"Out there? In front of all those people?" Dad asked, and I could see the little sweat beads starting to pop up on his forehead.

I don't think Dad would have ever agreed to go out there, but I couldn't keep quiet any longer. "Please, Dad. It would be so cool."

I know the look he gets on his face when he's about to give in and say yes. And it was on his face now. The promoter must have seen it too. He squealed his thanks and slapped Dad on the back. "I'll owe you big-time, buddy!" he said.

"If I survive . . ." Dad muttered, and then he walked toward the stage.

9
Larry

Cathy took me out of the backpack and I stood beside her and watched as Tom, looking as if someone was pushing him, managed to make it across the stage. Then he sat down at the piano and played the introduction to our song.

The audience was restless since Clementine was very late; a bunch of people were already moving up the aisles toward the exits. But they must have recognized the song Tom was playing, because when they heard it some of them turned back to applaud and a few others moved back to their seats. It looked like that made Tom feel a little better. I actually saw him sitting up straighter.

And then he was singing our song. Just the way he had been for weeks. Just like I heard him singing it in the shower earlier that night. He was doing fine. Really fine, in fact, until he got to the bridge.

Oh, no! He forgot the words. Then he forgot the tune. Then he stopped cold.

I could see his eyes darting around as he tried to remember the lyrics. He looked out at the audience. Thousands of eyes were staring back at him. He froze. Nothing came out of his mouth. His fingers couldn't play a note.

Cathy turned to Artie and shouted, "Do something!"

But Artie looked like a deer in the headlights too. There was no one else. It was up to me.

I took a deep breath and bolted between the legs of the stagehands, so fast nobody could stop me. White lightning! I had to save Tom.

I rushed out onto the stage toward the piano. When I got there, I used all the strength in my back legs to jump up on the piano bench. Actually, I was a little off the mark and plopped right onto Tom's lap. It was probably a good thing, though, because that got his attention. Up to that point he was still sitting there petrified. Still staring out at the thousands of faces staring back at him.

I know it was a completely crazy thing for me to do. But I couldn't help it. Leaning into the microphone the way I'd seen some of my favorite singers do it, I belted out the words we sang zillions of times around the house. And as I sang the song in my biggest voice, Tom remembered the words (thank heaven for miracles) and started to sing too. We sounded smooth.

When we finished I expected whistles and cheers. But the audience didn't move. Worse than that, their mouths were hanging open. Not like what dogs do when our tongues hang out of the side of our mouths and we pant. No. It seemed as if they weren't breathing at all.

Then, all at once, they screamed! And cheered and hollered and yelled.

I wanted to take a bow. Or, at least, to prance around the stage and show off. But now the people rose out of their seats and in a massive group they raced toward the stage, shouting.

"The dog must be a ventriloquist's dummy!"

"No, a little person in a costume!"

"A hologram!"

"A puppet!"

"A robot!"

"How did he do it?"

They scrambled up the stairs to the stage but luckily, before they could get to me, Cathy managed to run past all the security guards backstage and snatch me up. And Artie hustled Tom away from the oncoming crowd, shouting, "Let's get out of here before they start a riot!"

As we drove down the hill in Tom's truck, we saw the limos of Clementine and her band driving up the hill. They didn't know what they were in for.

10
Cathy

The next morning it felt like the whole world had turned upside down. Larry's singing at the Hollywood Bowl had been on the evening news, so reporters were calling. There were even a bunch of them with cameras and microphones on our front lawn!

While Dad was getting more and more nervous about the people out there, Larry was strutting around, thrilled to be the center of attention. I thought it was pretty great too! I mean, reporters and photographers were at our house, wanting to talk to us, to take pictures of us. When had that ever happened to a kid like me?

After a while, Larry sat down at the kitchen table and tried to hold a pen between his paws. I walked over to see what he was so busy doing.

"What's that?" I asked, looking at the paper he'd been using.

"I know," he said, a little embarrassed. "It's my first try at an *L*. Not too great. But I'll get it. When they ask for my autograph, I need to be ready." Then he smiled a big toothy doggy smile.

When the phone rang, I answered; it took me a minute to realize it was my best friend Lily, because she was shrieking.

"You are way famous!" she shouted. "Your dog is totally a star! I am so proud to be your friend. I saw people from TV standing on your lawn. Cath, please go out there and wave to the cameras. This is the coolest thing that ever happened to anyone I know!"

That's why I like Lily. She thinks even the craziest things that happen to me are great. So before Dad could stop me, I opened the front door just a little bit and slipped outside so I could see the news cameras up close and get a real sense of what was going on.

The second the reporters spotted me, they rushed up and stuck their microphones in my face. "Did you know Larry could sing?" "What else can he do?" "Is he going to sing again?" "Can he come out and talk to us?" they asked, all of them talking at once.

"Well," I said, and all the reporters got quiet and pushed their microphones toward me. I heard the *click-click-click* of a bunch of cameras taking my picture. So I brushed my bangs out of my eyes and then announced: "We were really happy to find out our dog Larry could talk and sing and also help my dad write songs. Larry's even more fun to have around now and he's helped my dad finally finish songs that were sitting in a drawer for years and . . ." That was when I felt my dad's hand on my shoulder pulling me back into the house.

"I just wanted to see what it felt like to be famous for a minute," I explained.

"No more," Dad said. "You can't encourage those people. Otherwise, they'll never go away and the neighbors will be miserable."

"But—" I tried to object.

"You will stay inside," Dad said, his eyes getting very big the way they do when he's upset.

And then the phone rang again, and it was my mother going bananas. She and her boyfriend Richard had been watching the news when, there on her TV screen, she saw me chatting away with the reporters. Mom said she rushed to the phone to call me.

"Pack your bag. You are not staying there to be a part

of that insanity," she said to me. "I don't know how he did that. Made it look as if our dog could sing. But whatever the trick is, you are not and will not be a part of it."

"Uh, Mom," I said. "I just heard the beep for call waiting and I–"

"Don't you dare put me on hold," she said, just as I did.

"Hi," said a woman's voice. "This is Linda Adams from IMA–International Musical Artists. I was at the Hollywood Bowl last night and I'd like to come over and meet with Tom Foster. IMA handles every big rock act in the world and I'm sure he'd like to us to represent him. I can make him a megastar within a year," she said.

"Megastar!" I said as Dad grabbed the phone.

"Look, I don't know who you are," Dad said. "But this whole thing has really gone far enough. You're nice to call but I'm not interested."

"But I am, I am, I am, I am," Larry said, panting and jumping up the way he does when he wants to go out for a walk and he sees me holding his leash.

Dad put his finger to his lips to shush Larry and listened while the lady on the phone kept talking. "No," Dad said into the phone, trying to stop her. "We don't want to be the biggest act in the world."

"We do-o-o-o-o," Larry howled.

I joined in. "We do-o-o-o-o. Daddy, at least go and meet with her," I begged.

Dad held the phone to his chest.

"Oh, come on, Tom," Larry said.

"Just hear what she has to say," I begged.

"What's one little meeting?" Larry asked, followed by his most pathetic whimper.

Dad sighed and put the phone to his ear. "Okay . . . Okay . . . What time tomorrow?" As he wrote down a time and an address, he didn't see Larry and me high-fiving each other behind his back.

11
Larry

"Your act rules, Tom," Linda said as we sat in her office. "Especially that gimmick of the little white dog. Tom, you are going to be a huge star, and however you do that thing with the dog, I'd definitely leave it in. Especially the part where you get him to jump up on the piano bench. Is that a remote control you have or something?"

Tom looked down at his shoes, while I forced myself to stay quiet. It was something I'd been doing very well for years.

"So, I think you should start at a little club like the Roxy," Linda said in what sounded to me like a phony sweet voice. "Maybe for a week or so while you break in the act. Get the kinks out, so to speak."

"We don't have an act," Tom said. "And I don't want to

have an act either. I just want to write my songs and let somebody else sing them."

"And you can do that. More than in your wildest dreams," Linda said, smiling at him. "But first you have to make a name for yourself. And right now, having little Larry as your partner is the best way to do it."

"Blondie," I blurted out. "You'd better hold off on calling me 'little Larry.' Because when Larry and Tom hit the big time, there'll be nobody bigger."

Linda gasped and looked at me, shaking her head, and then looked at Tom and laughed. "I don't know how you make him talk like that but I don't care. Because the whole world is going to love you two. Concerts, movies, maybe your own TV show."

"Forget it!" Tom said. "The other night was a horrible experience. I told you on the phone it was a one-time-only performance. And I meant what I said!"

But Cathy knew just what to do next. First she smiled her biggest smile at him. Then she announced, "Daddy, it won't be horrible. This time you'll be ready. This time you'll rehearse. You'll have an act. And you and Larry will be the biggest stars in the world."

"Yee-hah!" I started jumping all around with joy. Okay,

maybe I should have waited for Tom to say something. But I was so excited I couldn't help myself. "When do we start?"

Linda knew when to take yes for an answer. "A week from Saturday," she said. Then she laughed. "I can't believe I just talked to a dog!"

And before Tom could say anything, we were an act!

12
Cathy

The next day at school was wild. Everyone had seen me on TV and they crowded around me at my locker wanting to know everything about it. "When did you find out your dog could talk?" "What does it feel like to be able to talk to him?" "You were on TV! We saw you on TV!"

"Okay, Cathy," Derek said with a sneer. "What's the secret?"

"What secret?" I asked.

"How do they do the magic trick with the dog?"

"He really talks," I told him.

Derek just rolled his eyes to heaven. "Yeah, sure. I saw your dad's lips move," he said. "He does the voice, right?"

"Larry has his own voice," I said.

"No way!" he said. And he laughed.

The other kids started to laugh as I slammed my locker shut. That was when Lily came up behind me.

"Don't pay attention to Derek. You know what a dork he is."

"You believe me, don't you, Lily? You know it's no trick."

"Sure, Cathy. I totally believe you. It's so cool!" Lily said and we walked to the cafeteria together.

The rest of the day was the same. Some kids thought it was awesome, and others didn't believe it was real. But I told myself it didn't matter because I knew by four o'clock I'd be at rehearsal. My job was to keep everybody organized.

When I got to the studio, Dad and Larry were practicing their steps. Five, six, seven, eight . . . The sight of the two of them out there on the floor twirling and dancing while they sang made me laugh so much my stomach hurt. And if you don't think it's funny, picture your own dad and your own dog learning to do dance routines together. I love Dad, but he's kind of clumsy. And who would have ever imagined that Larry would be so graceful? It was as if he'd been waiting for this moment his whole life.

Jamie, the choreographer, was crazy about Larry from the start. He was not so crazy about Dad, whose name he kept getting wrong.

"Uh, Tim," he said to Dad, "perhaps you should just move from side to side during this verse while Larry has a solo?"

"Call me Tom," my dad said, nodding. He stepped back while the choreographer taught Larry his solo, which included not just some heavy-duty dance steps, but a backflip. And Larry mastered it all in less than a minute.

"Whoa! This mutt is magnificent," Artie said, elbowing me. Dad had insisted that Artie be hired as the musical director of the act. Poor Artie still hadn't gotten past his shock that Larry could talk, and every now and then he'd kind of cluck his tongue in amazement and say, "I can't believe what I'm hearing."

Greg the piano player was great, and I liked Jamie even though he kept getting Dad's name wrong. Artie had written some arrangements that made Dad and Larry sound good too. It was amazing. They were starting to be a real act!

I didn't like Linda, though. She came in with some

hats and jackets she thought "the guys" should wear on-stage. The hats were sparkly, glittery, silver baseball caps with *T* and *L* on the front, but she thought they should wear them backward. And the jackets were short little bolero things. Dad couldn't even get his on. But when I put the jacket and hat on Larry, everyone went wild over how cute he looked.

"Well, we'd certainly better rethink these outfits," said Jamie, trying not to laugh. "Ted looks like one of the elephants in *Fantasia*!"

"That's *Tom* who looks like an elephant," Dad said. Then he sighed. "Look, maybe I wasn't cut out for this. I'm a guy who likes being behind the scenes and I . . ."

Just then Larry jumped on the table and in one big gesture brushed the silver hats and jackets to the floor.

"First of all," Larry announced, "we are not going to agree to a costume until we find one that looks great on both of us. And will everyone kindly get his name right? He is Tom. Not Ted. Not Tim. Tom! Anyone who can't remember that can work somewhere else!"

Everyone got quiet after that. Dad's jaw even un-clenched a little.

"Relax, Tom. We're gonna be great!" Larry said. "And,

Linda, Tom and I decide what we wear and what we sing. And we're going to rock the audience right out of their seats. Hats or no hats.

"You can do this, Tom, I know you can," Larry said in a voice that sounded like he got it from a character in one of those old movies he watched at night when he had the TV remote to himself. "We're going to go out there as youngsters, but we've got to come back as stars."

"I love that!" my dad said, throwing an arm around Larry. "That's brilliant!"

"Ahhh, I stole it from the movie *42nd Street*," Larry admitted. "Which is where I picked up all my dancing skills, by the way."

Jamie chuckled at that. "Hah! Too bad Todd didn't watch it with you; it would have made *my* life easier."

"That's *Tom*," Larry said.

"I knew that," Jamie said. But I was pretty sure he didn't.

13
Larry

Tonight was opening night. I was super-relaxed, but Tom was super-shaky. Linda hired a makeup person, and the nice lady put a little blusher on Tom's cheeks, which made him sneeze.

We had to rehearse every day all day for the whole two weeks before we opened at the Roxy because Tom was a wreck. Poor guy! He would forget from one day to the next what we learned and then he'd fall apart saying he couldn't do it and I'd have to go into my pep talk again to get him back into it. But I felt bad for him because he was trying so hard. The man has two left feet, as they say. Fortunately all four of my feet are very synchronized. I even started doing a few hip-hop moves.

Since that night at the Hollywood Bowl, we had been in-terviewed by a few local magazines and newspapers because Linda said people needed to know about our show. Just a few people around here knew I was for real—now we were ready to tell the whole world.

Our outfits were very hot. Tom wore a tux made out of satin and a ruffled shirt and a glittering bow tie. Since I look as if I'm already ruffled, I didn't need the shirt, just the tie.

I started going over the steps in my head and some of the lyrics to the songs. One song was called "Sleepin' at the Foot of the Bed." Another was "I Want to Hold Your Paw." And the best one was "In the Doghouse with You." We were going to end with a song we'd written called "Going Out on the Town." My favorite part of that was at the end when Tom played a real fast version and I did some great moves on the piano.

Through the intercom in the dressing room we could hear the hum of the audience pouring into the Roxy. It made Tom a little queasy. Not me. Even though I've heard it's not professional to do this, I crept out of the dressing room and peeked through the curtain to see how many people were out there. There wasn't an empty seat in the place.

I spotted Cathy in a lacy pink dress she'd gotten just for tonight. I even caught sight of Peggy, Cathy's mom, in the back with her boyfriend, Richard. Richard has always treated me like a dog, making comments to Cathy like, "No dogs on the couch, please." Yeah, well, after tonight we'll see who can sit on the couch and who can't.

"Five minutes," I heard the stage manager holler. I went back to see how Tom was doing.

"You hanging in there, buddy?" I asked, because even with the blusher Tom was looking a little pale.

But his big blue eyes sparkled when he stood up. He straightened his tie and said, "I'm doing this for Cathy. So let's get out there and knock them dead."

"Places!" the stage manager hollered so loud it made Tom jump. He picked me up for a little good-luck hug and we walked to the edge of the curtain. The houselights went to half and a hush fell over the audience. Then the room went dark and the announcer's voice rang out like a bell:

"Ladies and gentlemen. Please welcome . . . Tom and Lar-rrrry!"

The cheers were deafening. When the lights came up, we were at the piano, Tom seated at the keyboard and me on top of the baby grand, whose shiny surface made a perfect dance floor for me. Tom had to play the introduction to the song three times because the audience, filled with our friends, was going so insane just from seeing us up there in our costumes. And then we sang in close harmony.

I like to wag my tail for you
Well, it's the least that I can do
So please don't tell me that I can't
Each time I see you, girl, I pant
Oh, I'm a very lucky dog
Arf, arf, arf, arf

After the first few choruses the audience sang along with the "arf, arf, arf, arf" part.

Once, while I was doing a really tough dance move, I looked right over at Cathy. She was grinning the biggest grin I'd ever seen on anybody. She looked so pretty too, sitting back there between her mom and her mom's anti-dog boyfriend.

Never mind! I was blazing too hot to care about small-time dog-phobic people like him now. Every move I made, every sound out of my cute little white throat was being heard by, worshipped by and adored by the crowd. At the end of the first number they jumped to their feet, screaming and hollering, and they pretty much stood—rocking and swaying and singing along with every song we sang—for the rest of the night. The building felt as if it could leave the ground and take off into space. And I was the pilot.

Oh, don't get me wrong; Tom was the co-pilot. But let's face it, when a man writes songs and sings, that's not news. But when a *dog* writes songs, sings them, dances to them and throws in a back flip or two—baby, that's huge! And I was on my way to being the King of Rock and Roll!

14
Cathy

After that night everyone was talking about "Tom and Larry." Dad was really surprised when he flipped through the TV channels and saw himself on the news. Not just the news where we lived but all over the country. Even all over the world. Some newscasters were speaking in languages we couldn't understand. But no matter what the language, the words "Larry the Dog" always came through loud and clear.

One show actually had a panel of experts talking about what had happened. The first one was a veterinarian from Florida who said that after working with dolphins who could say words like "Ma" and "Pa," he wouldn't be surprised if a dog could say a few words here and there. But sing a whole song? Never. It had to be a trick.

Another show had a ventriloquist named Sammy, who had a dummy named Arfie—a floppy kind of doggy puppet. Sammy took Arfie out of a box and put him on his lap and made him look kind of like a real dog and made him sing. Everyone agreed that my dad might be a ventriloquist. I guess some people didn't want to believe the truth.

But other people did believe it and they were furious at their own dogs for not being able to sing. They tried to get their dogs to sing anything. "Come on, Trixie. You can do it. Just a few notes." And then the owners would sing the songs themselves, trying to get their Labradors or their Cocker Spaniels to sing along.

Their dogs just stared at them, heads cocked to the side the way dogs do. As if to say, "you are a nutcase!" But these dogs couldn't talk or sing. Only Larry could talk and could sing and write a song.

The reporters were back and they had photographers with them. This time they followed Larry and Dad and me everywhere we went. It was pretty embarrassing when they followed me to school. Lily stuck up for me when the other kids laughed. "You wish you were this famous," Lily said to Shannon when Shannon said it was lame to have your dog be a star.

The reporters followed Larry and me to the park and the whole time shouted questions.

"Hey, Larry, if you're for real, why don't you stop and talk to us?" But we knew if we stopped to talk to them there would be a riot, so we kept walking.

They even followed us to a fancy restaurant where we met Linda for lunch. (Of course we had to go someplace that had tables on the sidewalk so Larry could go too.) He looked so cute sitting up on his chair. Everything was fine until the waiter asked Larry if he needed a booster seat. That's when Larry lost it and glared at the waiter. "I may look small to you, but I'm perfectly capable of eating without the help of a height enhancer."

Linda tried to distract the reporters, who were writing down every word Larry said. "I want your readers to be the first to know," Linda announced in a slightly louder voice to get their attention, "that in response to the many requests for Tom and Larry to perform, I am booking them on a tour of the United States. Pretty soon they'll sing and dance and entertain the entire country."

The next week Dad and Larry were on the cover of *People* magazine. Some of the tabloids gossiped about whether or not Larry was dating a Maltese belonging to Courtney Mason. That was gross!

Even with that annoying stuff going on, Dad seemed to be having fun. It was like he was a kid again as they got their act ready for the tour. He loved the idea that he and Larry had their own bus; Dad stocked it with all kinds of food and music. Through it all, Larry was being his Larry self. Hamming it up. Singing out and smiling real big. He watched old music videos of 'N Sync and tried to teach Dad 'N Sync's dance steps. But Dad kept saying he was a musician, not a performer, and Larry finally gave up.

I was really hoping to go with them, at least for part of the tour, but Mom put a stop to that. "Absolutely not. You have school. You have your friends here. And I don't want you to spend any part of your childhood hanging out backstage!"

But she still took me to see them off on the day they left for the tour. I know Dad didn't want to leave me. Just before they got on the bus, Dad and Larry both came over to say good-bye to me. I tried hard not to cry because I felt so left out.

"We'll miss you so much," Dad said and he gave me a big warm Daddy hug. Larry gave me a little slurp on my cheek and then they both hopped onto the bus. When the doors closed behind them, I turned away so I wouldn't have to watch the bus drive off.

15
Larry

Wow! I'd heard a lot about what happens when rock stars go on tour, but I wasn't ready for it to happen to me. As we rode through the countryside to our first show in Pittsburgh, I watched everything from my perch at the bus window. (By the way, since I got to be a star, I had lots of people to pile up my pillows just the way I liked them.) And when I looked out the window, I saw people lined up on the edge of the road holding up signs they printed that said LARRY! STOP HERE! SING HERE! WE LOVE YOU LARRY! I was glad that Tom was sitting on the other side of the bus because I was afraid his feelings would be hurt if he saw they were all there clamoring for me.

When we got to the arena where we were performing that night, I couldn't believe my eyes. There, in big letters on a marquee twenty feet high, were the words TONIGHT! TOM

AND LARRY! SOLD OUT! We went inside to rehearse and all the workmen stopped what they were doing to watch me walk up on the stage. Okay, I was a little insulted when I heard one of the carpenters say to the guy next to him, "I bet Phil twenty bucks that little mutt can't really talk. I'm going to hang out backstage until I figure out their gimmick."

But then I smiled to myself because I knew he'd be waiting a long, long time. Sooner or later he'd have to admit I wasn't a gimmick. I was the real thing.

The night of the first show thousands of people were screaming my name! Oh, and Tom's name too. But they were mostly the "older" people. All the cool young people were there to see me.

I couldn't wait to call Cathy after the show and tell her what a hit we were. But Tom beat me to the phone. (The truth is I needed him to dial. My paws don't work too well on some touch-tone phones.)

"Hey, Cath!" Tom called to her. "We were great tonight, honey!"

I was in the background yelping, "Me next! I wanna talk. I wanna talk," but Tom was so excited, I couldn't get him to hold out the phone for me. "Pittsburgh loves Tom and Larry," I called over his shoulder.

"But I love Tom and Larry more," I could hear her say back.

"There were two thousand people out there tonight," he said to her. "What a crowd."

We called Cathy every night after the show to tell her how it was going. It was awesome the way in every new city the crowds were bigger than the one before.

Cathy said she let out a holler when she and her mother were watching television that night and they heard the newscasters talking about how people had been sleeping overnight in tents in front of the stadiums where we were playing just to be sure they could get tickets for our show.

But Cathy said she thought I went a little overboard when I was being interviewed. I looked right into the camera and with a big doggy grin said, "Watch out, world! Tom and Larry are going to be bigger than the Beatles!"

16
Cathy

When *"Tom and Larry"* finally got to LA to play The Forum, Richard pretended he had a cold so he wouldn't have to come to the concert with me and Mom. I knew it was a fake cold because he couldn't stand that Larry was now a huge star. But I couldn't wait to get to the concert. I hadn't seen either Dad or Larry in weeks and this was their first big performance in LA.

Dad sent me and Mom two tickets in the front row along with backstage passes so we could come back and see him after the show. When we got to the arena, I couldn't believe the crowds. Thousands of people chanting, "Tom! Tom! Tom! Larry! Larry! Larry!" I mean, Tom is my father. The guy who always walks around in a

T-shirt and forgets his keys every time he leaves the house. And Larry—well, before I knew he could talk, and sing, and dance, he was just my doggy. And now the two of them were big rock stars! I went to that concert feeling like the proudest girl on the planet.

Inside the auditorium I grabbed on to Mom's arm and we squeezed through the screaming people to get to our seats. No matter how many times Dad or Larry described how huge the crowds were for their concerts, I really never expected to see what I saw. And, whoa! It scared me a little. Okay, it scared me a lot. Even Mom looked a little freaked out.

When the lights went down, a roar went up from the crowd. Thousands of flashes went off like little explosions all over the auditorium. Everyone in the room seemed to know the lyrics to every Tom and Larry song. People stood and swayed back and forth, singing along with Dad and Larry.

Dad looked so sweet at the keyboard, plunking away at all their tunes. "Arf, arf, arf, arf," everyone sang along when Larry strutted back and forth and moved down to the front of the stage, so close that the kids in the audience could reach up and touch him.

A few seats from me a girl with hair down to her waist reached her arms out to the stage. She cried and screamed, "Larre-e-e-e-y, I love you! You're my dog!"

Hey, wait a second, I thought. Larry was *my* dog!

Once the show was over, Mom and I hurried to the backstage door but we were nearly trampled by all the fans who wanted to be the first ones to see Larry when he came out.

"Hey, I was standing there!" a girl with red hair hollered, and shoved me away. She pushed so hard that I fell backward and reached for Mom's arm to get my balance. And just as I did, the cord that held the laminated pass around my neck broke and I watched my backstage pass flutter to the ground. I tried to get to it, but the crowd moved in on us. Everyone wanted to push closer to the door; my pass was under their feet somewhere, but I knew I'd never find it.

The door opened and a guard in uniform appeared. "Nobody gets in without a pass," he grumbled.

"But Larry's my dog!" I said. "And Tom's my father!"

"Yeah, sure, girlie," the guard said to me. "That's what all the fans say." He looked right over my head.

"I swear, Larry's my dog," I tried again, tearfully.

Mom stood behind me. "It's true," she shouted to the guard over the noise. The guard didn't even look at us.

"It's useless, honey," Mom said. We turned to leave and I burst into tears. As Mom and I drove home, she turned up the radio. I was glad, because I was way too upset to talk.

17

Larry

Finally the tour was over. We had done shows in New York, Baltimore, Pittsburgh, Cleveland, Chicago, Milwaukee, Dallas, San Francisco, Seattle, Denver, Miami, Nashville and Atlanta. I was ready to be home. In fact, I was ecstatic to be home. I pranced all over the house, following Cathy from room to room, yammering away about all the stuff that happened on the tour that I might have forgotten to tell her on those nights Tom and I called.

"And then we did an encore and when it was over the whole audience jumped to their feet and we were out there bowing and saying, 'Thank you, thank you and . . .' "

I knew she had heard the stories a thousand times already, but she was nice enough to listen and then say, "Wow!" each time I told her. Most of the time I tried to sit quietly next to her on the floor wagging my tail while she did her homework or snuggle up with her when she watched her favorite TV shows. But I was having a hard time sitting still. I couldn't wait to get to the keyboard, switch on Tom's songwriting software and turn out a few more hits for our album.

One day an assistant from Linda's office came to the door. She yelled, "Fan mail!" then ran back to her station wagon, opened the tailgate and pulled out five huge bags, which Tom helped her lug into the living room.

"Dad, can I take a break from my math to help you open these?" Cathy asked.

"Sure," Tom said. "In fact, you can be the official opener for me because I've got to go to the supermarket to get food for dinner."

"Going to the market?" I asked, surprised. "We're famous now. Shouldn't you have somebody go for you?"

"C'mon, Larry," Tom said. "We're just a couple of guys who wrote a few okay songs. And to tell the truth, the only reason we fill those auditoriums has nothing to do with me. It's my singing dog."

"That's not true, Dad," Cathy objected. "You're a rock star too."

"Thanks, Pumpkin," he said, "but even rock stars have to eat. So I'll be back in a flash."

He grabbed his grocery list from under a magnet on the fridge and was gone. Cathy and I set to work going through those mailbags. The envelopes were addressed to Tom and Larry, Tom and Larry, Larry, Larry, Larry, Larry the Dog, to Larry the coolest dog on earth . . . "Oooh, let's open that one," I said. Cathy tore into it because paws weren't really meant for opening letters.

" 'Dear Larry, you are the coolest dog on earth,' " Cathy read. " 'When I saw your picture on the cover of *People* magazine, I tore it off and showed it to my dog Nelly, a boxer. I wanted her to see that if she would just work a little harder, maybe she could be on TV like you. I was surprised in the morning to see what Nelly had done to the picture. She has never done that on the floor before and she is ten.' "

"Oops," I said. "Hope that wasn't my fault."

" 'Dear Larry, we are starting a Larry Fan Club at our school. Will you send us some autographed pictures of you and that guy who plays the piano for you? You are a wonder. The Larry Lovers of Leonia, New Jersey.' "

Cathy looked over at me. "Boy, I'm glad my dad didn't see that one."

"Me too," I said, stretching out and sighing happily. "You can understand why it might look that way, as if Tom was just my band. When I'm out there, all eyes are on me. I am a wonder!"

"Hey! Look at this stamp. Some of these letters are coming from Japan, and some of them from Europe, and this one's from Israel!" Cathy said.

"A worldwide wonder," I said happily, hoping Tom would get home soon and start cooking dinner.

"Yo, everybody!" Artie hollered as he knocked on the door. Cathy hurried to answer and I followed behind. "Look what I got," he said as Cathy opened the door. "Tickets to take all of us to see *The Lion King* next week."

The Lion King! I had been wanting to see it for a long time. All those knockout costumes and the great music. I couldn't wait.

"Awesome, Artie," Cathy said.

"Three seats in row five," Artie said, grinning proudly.

I counted on my toes, trying to figure out who the three was going to be. Me, Cathy, Artie. Me, Tom, Cathy. "Uh, Artie," I said, "I believe we're a party of four, not three."

Artie looked at me for what felt like a full minute before he broke into a smile. "We?" he said, then laughed a big guffaw of a laugh. "We? Isn't that adorable? The mutt here thinks they'd let him into a theater."

"I beg your pardon," I said. "I have just been inside some of the biggest and most important theaters in this country. And every seat was filled because I was performing in those theaters."

"Yeah, well, on that side of the footlights, you're allowed," Artie said. "But they can't let you come to a show. Some people would never sit in a theater seat again if they knew some dog had been sittin' in it."

Artie laughed again while Cathy only sighed. I walked back into the living room where the mailbags were sitting and suddenly all those letters lost their charm for me.

I don't think people realize how they humiliate dogs every day of their lives. Why is it people think we're not clean enough to go wherever we want? To supermarkets? To restaurants? I'm not dirty. I'm cleaner than a lot of people I've met. And then, to make it even worse, because they can't take us inside, they make us wait in the car. It's hot in there. And way boring. Maybe if they left the radio and the air-conditioning on . . . But, no, we're just expected to wait out there in the parking lot.

Disgraceful!

And how about going to the movies? Do you know how many movies I've missed? *Air Bud. 101 Dalmatians.* Sure, they have DVDs. But Cathy already saw most of those movies in the theater. So she never rents the videos, which means I don't get to see them at all. And, while I'm on the subject, what about my not being able to go to Disneyland? Do you know I've never even been on a roller coaster? Or a merry-go-round? I've missed all the fun.

When Artie left, Cathy went back to her math and I sat alone for a long time in front of the mailbags. Okay, I thought, reading fan letters has got to cheer me up. So I'll go for one more.

Cathy had removed a big stack from the first bag, and I randomly picked one letter out. By holding it between my paws I was able to slit the envelope with one of my longer teeth on the side. Then I spread the letter on the floor.

It was printed out on a computer. It was short. It said,

WE'RE WATCHING YOU, LARRY.
AND WE SURE DON'T LIKE WHAT WE SEE.
BE CAREFUL. WE'RE NOT GOING TO
PUT UP WITH YOU MUCH LONGER!

18
Cathy

The next morning I was still singing all of the songs from *The Lion King* while I painted the sign for my booth at the school fair next month. I was in charge of the Dunk-A-Dad booth, and Dad had volunteered to sit over the giant tub of water while the kids tried to hit the bull's-eye and make him fall into it. The doorbell rang and I leaned my brush against the paint can and ran to answer it.

"Hi, Mom." I was surprised to see her because she didn't usually come over to Dad's house.

"Hi, Pumpkin," she said as I gave her a hug. Mom washes her hair every day with a lemony shampoo and I love the way she smells. She was grinning as she stood in the doorway of Dad's house.

"I have some really good news," she said, "which you may not think is good news, but after a while I think you'll see it is."

Uh-oh, I thought. This sounds scary.

She came into Dad's living room, walking past the bags of fan mail, and sat down. "Richard asked me to marry him last night and I said yes. I wanted you to be the first one to know."

"When?" I barely croaked that out of my throat.

"In a few months," she said.

She must have seen my eyes fill up with tears. My stomach was in knots. I wanted to scream, "No, no, no, no, no! Go back with Dad and get rid of Richard!" But what I said was, "I'm glad for you, Mom."

"I know you'd prefer it if your dad and I were to-gether, honey, but I don't think that could ever work."

Larry, who had been napping upstairs, trotted down. He rushed over to lick Mom in greeting.

"Hey, Peggy," he said and she ruffled his fur.

I must have looked really sad because Larry, who hasn't been acting very much like a dog at all lately, ac-tually jumped into my lap.

"Mom's getting married," I told him, trying not to cry.

"Oh," Larry said. Then he added, politely, "Congratulations."

I guess Mom saw that both Larry and I weren't thrilled, but she tried to keep everything light. "You'll help me plan the wedding. And we'll shop for a beautiful dress for you to wear."

"I don't wear dresses," Larry joked. "I'm a guy." I forced a smile, trying hard to hold back the tears. "Whoa," Larry said as it hit him. "So you're marrying the dog hater?" he asked.

"Richard's not really a dog hater," Mom said. "He's just not used to dogs. But he's trying."

Larry just sighed and all three of us sat quietly.

"I'll leave you two alone for now. But I know you'll be happy when you get used to the idea," Mom said as she was leaving.

When she was in the car and Larry knew she couldn't hear him, he said, "You wanna bet?" Then he looked at me. "You okay?" he asked.

"Sort of," I said, but Larry knows me better than that.

"This calls for a trip to the park," he said. He ran to get his leash and brought it to me in his mouth the way he used to before any of us knew he could talk. He even sat still while I put the leash on him, something he never did in the days before he talked to us. That's when I knew that deep down he was still my good friend.

At first I barely noticed the signs pasted to the lamp-posts leading into the park announcing an important meeting. A protest meeting, it said. The words "Our very way of life is at stake" were in big black letters. But the signs weren't high up where I could read them. They were low, down around my knees. When I stooped down to read what the signs said, Larry kept pulling on his leash. "C'mon. I see a Frisbee with my name on it sailing through the air!" he shouted.

"Hey, it's Cathy," I heard someone say. When I looked around, I saw Lily and my other friend Abigail. "And her awesome dog!" Abigail said.

"Hey, Larry, how'd you like being on tour?" Abigail asked.

"It was pretty cool," Larry said. "Wherever we went, everyone was cheering for me and calling my name!"

"Did you miss us at all?" Lily laughed.

"Sure, I did. I couldn't wait to get back so I could hang around with you and listen in on all your secrets."

"Like what?" Abigail asked warily.

"Like hearing you tell Cathy that of all the boys in

sixth grade you liked Jack Singer the best. And hearing Lily say she hoped her mom didn't find out she cut school to go to the movies."

"Larry, you wouldn't dare tell our secrets!" Abigail shrieked.

"Now that I can talk, you never know," Larry teased.

"He's joking," I said, hoping to convince Lily and Abigail he was only kidding, but I could tell they weren't too sure.

At dinner that night Dad said, "I heard about your mom and Richard getting married." He looked as sad as I felt. "But I've got news that should cheer you up. Larry and I are performing at a benefit show for a charity in San Diego this weekend. We want you to come with us. Whaddaya say?"

"Yes! Yes! Yes!" I said and Dad grinned.

"I sure wish we could take you to all of our shows, honeybunch," he told me. "It would make it so much more fun for Larry and me. But this is a quick trip. We're even flying down there instead of using our bus."

The next day, I packed jeans and my TOM AND LARRY T-shirt because that was what everyone wore to Dad and Larry's shows. We all went in Artie's station wagon to the airport and checked our bags at the curb. Then the skycap who was checking us in said, "And did you want to put that dog in cargo, or carry him on?"

We all froze. Dad hadn't even thought about it.

"Cargo? Uh, I don't think so. I didn't bring a crate," Dad said.

I looked at Larry. "Lend me money for a taxi," Larry said. "Because I'm going home. I am not getting on that plane."

"The airline will provide you with a crate that fits right under the seat," the skycap said to Dad.

"Under the seat," Larry said. "Under the seat? Do you know who I am?"

"I sure do," the skycap said, smiling. "Everyone knows who you are, Larry, but those are the airline rules. Dogs in cargo or under the seat."

"Not this dog, friend!" Larry announced. By now a line of people were behind us, saying, "Could you move it along up there?"

The skycap shrugged. "Sorry," he said to Dad. "Maybe you big rock stars ought to fly in private airplanes, 'cause no airline's gonna let that dog have a seat, I'm telling you right now."

Dad looked at his watch. There wasn't time to do anything but get right on the airplane before it left with-out us.

"Larry, we have no choice. The concert is in two hours," Dad said.

"How would you like to be stuffed in a crate?" Larry shouted as the skycap took a crate from behind the counter and handed it to Dad. Larry just shook his head miserably and climbed into it. As we walked through the airport, I could hear Larry muttering. Especially when we passed the newsstand and there was *Us Weekly* with his picture on the cover.

"Look at that!" he hollered out. "Is this some kind of a cruel joke? I'm a star and a prisoner at the same time!"

As the airplane took off, Larry jabbered inside his crate about how someday he was going to become the president of the world and all dogs would have the rights they deserved. But after a while I didn't pay attention to him because all I could think about was my mom's wed-ding.

When the seat belt sign went off, I slid down to the floor in front of my seat and looked into the crate. Larry took one look at my face and he knew something was wrong. He stuck his nose up against the crate. I put my finger up to his nose and he licked it a few times sweetly.

"Is this about the wedding?" he asked. I nodded.

"Well, maybe they'll let me be the ring bearer and I can carry the ring down the aisle in my teeth and drop it, so they have to call the whole thing off."

That really made me laugh. I couldn't help it. It was so silly. Then I started to cry. I leaned into the crate and Larry licked the tears off my cheeks. The way he did in the days when he was just my dog. After I looked around to make sure none of the flight attendants could see, I opened the crate, and Larry stepped into my arms so I could bury my crying face in his furry little body. It was just what I needed.

19
Larry

After we came back from San Diego, Cathy tried hard to be cheerful, but I knew she was very sad. Every day I waited for her to come home from school so I could cheer her up.

That day as I looked out the window, my heart suddenly started pounding a mile a minute. I know there have been lots of songs written over the years to describe the feeling I had at that moment. I think it's called love at first sight, and it hits you like getting a Frisbee in the face.

Outside, in front of our house, was the most amazing-looking girl Maltese I had ever seen. Actually, I think I might have seen her before at the park or somewhere, so maybe this was love at second or third sight.

And then, she stepped right up onto our porch! I nudged

the door open with my nose and we stood there snout-to-snout. "May I help you?" I asked.

She smiled and said, "Hello, Larry. We've played in the same park a few times but you probably never noticed me. I'm Maggie."

I guess I finally have to admit to you that my being a talking dog is not so special. The truth is (and I hope you're sitting down for this) that all dogs can talk. In fact, when humans aren't listening, dogs actually speak words to one another all the time. But right from the time we are born into our litter we make a serious pact not to let humans know. I guess it's pretty obvious that I broke that pact because of my quick temper.

Right now it was pretty special just to have Maggie here and talking only to me. I mean, I was about as melted as a marshmallow over a campfire. She had the biggest brownest eyes.

"Wanna go for a walk?" she asked.

"Absolutely," I said, wondering how Cathy would feel if I wasn't there when she got home. "Oh, Cathy will be fine," I told myself as I walked down the porch steps to the sidewalk with Maggie. I felt the warm sun beating down on us as we moved side-by-side down the street. I couldn't help but steal sidelong glances at Maggie. She had little yellow bows above each ear that set off her stunning face.

"I've been noticing you for a long time," she said. "Long before you went and told the world that you could talk."

"Really?" I said, trying to be cool and cover the fact that her words were music to my floppy ears.

"But today I'm not here just for me," she said. And my stomach lurched at the change in tone of her voice. "I guess you can imagine how all the other dogs feel about you revealing the secret. Blurting out that you can talk."

I nodded, for once not knowing what to say.

"They're threatened by what you did, Larry. And you can understand why they would be."

"Look, Maggie." I tried to reason with her. "I didn't mention anyone else. Not even one other dog. Just me. I would never reveal the secret of dogdom to the world. I swear it."

"They don't believe that, Larry. Dogs were called to a protest meeting last night," she said. "You may have seen the signs posted on the lampposts."

"I did."

Then she stopped walking and put her paw on mine. "Dogs from all over the city snuck out of their houses through their doggy doors when their humans were asleep because it was that important for them to be there. To talk about how to deal with what you did!"

I was scared now. "Why?"

"Because they don't trust you, Larry. And trust is the ultimate quality in a dog. Remember Old Dog Trey? Remember B-I-N-G-O? Remember Snoopy? Even Dennis the Menace's dog, Ruff! All trustworthy. But not you. Well, everyone is furious, to say the least."

"But I would never—" I tried to explain.

Maggie cut me off. "It's too late for that now. I have to tell you what happened last night."

"Okay," I said sheepishly.

"Well, Solomon, a wise old Shar-Pei, ran the meeting. And he started by saying that we'd all have to stop you before you ruined our lives forever. And then Stuart, the Wheaten Terrier whose humans live at the beach . . . You've met him, haven't you, Larry? He's usually very levelheaded. But you've got him worried too. He said our lives may soon be no better than humans'. That dogs may have to get jobs. That dogs may have to trudge through life in a 'man eat man' world. He thinks you could create that kind of damage."

"But I didn't! I wouldn't!" I pleaded.

"The reports they've heard on KNIN have made all the dogs question that, Larry."

KNIN is the dog radio station and I listen to it when no one else is around. KNIN operates on a frequency that only dogs can hear. It's how we communicate with greater dogdom. We tune in and hear dog news and dog music and dog weather (they never say it's raining cats and dogs). KNIN announces which parks allow dogs to run free without a leash. And what to avoid during flea season. And which neighborhoods have tough dogs who like to jump out and scare the smaller breeds. It's very useful information.

"That's where Adolph, a very angry Doberman, heard about what you had done, Larry, and he howled that he wanted them to find a way to do away with you completely."

"Oh, no," I gasped.

"A cry went up from the others. Coco the Poodle piped up, 'No! Dogs don't behave that way. Dogs are loyal. Dogs are loving. We just have to retrain him.'

"But," Maggie went on, "not one of them believed it would be possible to retrain you after seeing you on TV shows and reading in the paper how the Tom and Larry star is rising in the sky."

"Uh, it's Larry and Tom," I said, correcting her.

Maggie sighed. "See! That proves they were probably right. I thought I could help you. I told them I could be your bodyguard. I could keep you from causing any more trouble. The others in the room laughed at that idea. There was a German Shepherd, a Great Dane and a Siberian Husky who said even *they* wouldn't try to guard you. Why should they believe a dainty little fluffy female like me would have influence over you? 'Because he and I are the same breed,' I told them. 'Because I understand him. I'll see to it that his big ego doesn't threaten the rest of dogdom.' "

She said the other dogs thought about it for a moment, then talked among themselves. "They said, 'Nobody can resist the powers of the beautiful Maggie,' " she told me, blushing. "But others clucked their tongues at the silliness of the idea that I could have any influence whatsoever over a lost cause like you."

Maggie told me that Solomon commanded everyone to silence. Then he looked deeply into her eyes and said, "Margaret, you are hereby assigned the job of serving as the bodyguard to that impossible Larry. You must never leave his side, no matter what happens. Do you swear to carry out those orders?"

"I do," Maggie said.

Whoa! Talk about good news coming out of bad. Maggie would never leave my side. How did a no-good guy like me get so lucky?

20
Cathy

Dad missed being home with me, so he decided he and Larry should take an extended break from touring. After Dad told Linda "no performing" for a while, Dad and Larry and I spent lots of time together: Working on my Dunk-A-Dad booth for the school fair, taking long car rides and playing in the park.

Larry had been hanging out at the park with that pretty Maltese I'd seen flirting with him, but today was just for our family. We were going to the mall. Dad said I should do a little window-shopping, since my birthday was in a few weeks and I could start thinking about what birthday gift I wanted.

We had been walking for just a few minutes when we came upon one of those pet stores that had a pen of cute little puppies in the window.

"Awww, how cute!" I started tapping my finger against the glass, trying to get the attention of a scruffy-looking Beagle.

"Don't annoy him like that," Larry yelled at me so sharply I spun around, surprised. "It's bad enough they stick him in the window like he's a piece of meat for sale. At least give him his dignity."

That's when Dad jumped in. "What's the matter with you, Larry? Cathy was just saying hello to the dog. It's no more than a little wave. Like saying have a nice day."

"How could he have a nice day? Look at him. The poor thing is saying, 'I beg you. Take me . . . Please get me out of this darned window.' The whole thing is humiliating."

"But the pet store finds good homes for them this way, don't they?" Dad asked. "What's wrong with putting puppies where people can see how cute they are?"

"Why you . . . you . . ." Larry's white face was red with anger. "You canineist!" he said, pointing a paw at Dad.

"If that's supposed to be an insult," Dad said, "you'd better take it back right now. I can look back over my life and say with no fear of contradiction that some of my best friends have been dogs!"

"Ha!" Larry said. "As long as they ate in the laundry room."

"Your bowl was on a mat in the kitchen!" Dad screamed.

"On the floor, not on the table."

"I thought it was easier for you to reach."

"You couldn't stand the smell of that crummy dog food!" Larry said. "Well, guess what? Neither could I."

"How was I supposed to know that?" Dad asked.

"Okay, you two," I said, trying to be the referee and stop the fight.

"You, my friend, are barking up the wrong tree," Dad said.

"Poor choice of phrase," Larry shot back.

But Dad ignored that and kept on ranting. "Look, I'm the one who goes on the road with a dog, shares billing with a dog, hangs around with a dog and—"

"Because you wouldn't have an act or hit songs *without* that certain dog," Larry cut him off. People in the mall were snickering as they passed Dad and Larry arguing. I guess most of them had probably seen Larry on TV, and now seeing him hollering at his partner made them chuckle and elbow one another. "And it would certainly not be the classy act it is now if I hadn't been the idea man behind it," Larry sneered.

"You're the idea man?" Dad said, now as angry as I'd

ever seen him. *"You are the idea man?* Now that is truly funny!"

"If I left it up to you, we'd be doing 'How Much Is that Doggy in the Window.' Do you have any idea how mortifying that would have been for me?" Larry asked. "No! Of course you don't. Why would you? Dogs have 'waggly tails' and are 'for sale,' and that to you is funny! If I hadn't threatened to walk if you put that in the act, you actually would have used that song! And if I *had* walked, where would you be? Nowhere. And why is it every time Linda calls with an offer for us to go on the road, you find a way to turn it down?" Larry said, his ears practically pink with anger. "And you always give her some lame excuse, like 'Ooooh, Linda, we need a big chunk of time just to unwind. I can't go away for that long. My daughter needs me.' "

I didn't know that's what Dad said to Linda.

"Wimpy excuses! Let's take Cathy out of school and bring her along. She can play the tambourine in the band. You don't need talent for that!" Larry said.

Whoa! Now he was insulting *me!*

I was just about to say something when I saw Artie running across the mall toward us, out of breath.

"Hey you three!" he shouted, waving a letter in his

hand. "Look at this. It was sent to Linda and she's been going bananas trying to find you."

Larry glared at Artie as Dad took the envelope and opened it. "This is the seal of the White House!" Dad said to me, his eyes wide. "It's an invitation for me and Larry to perform there in two weeks. At a state dinner for the President and the First Lady and some foreign dignitaries!"

Larry immediately jumped up and raised his paw and Artie slapped it with his hand. They danced all around the mall.

"The White House," Artie sang, amazed.

They were twirling and laughing until Dad looked at the invitation again and stopped in mid-twirl. "Wait!" he said. "I can't be there that night."

"What do you mean?" Larry asked.

"Look at the date," Dad said. And then I looked at it and my heart sank.

Larry sputtered angrily. "This is what I mean about you, Tom. You're *not* going to the White House because you have some kind of scheduling conflict? What else could be happening on March third that would make you say no to the President of the United States?"

"It's Cathy's birthday and her party," Dad said, putting an arm around me. "It's been planned for at least a month. The invitations are already out to all the kids and we've ordered the cake."

Larry just shook his head and said, "Oh, brother. Gimme a break!"

21
Larry

Hey, correct me if I'm wrong, but isn't it true that birthdays come along every year, and a chance to sing at the White House is a once-in-a-lifetime experience? So even if Cathy was upset (and I personally believed she was being a little babyish about the whole thing), I thought it was silly to miss the greatest honor ever. Especially for a bunch of balloons and that dumb pointy birthday party hat they always put on me and some gooey cake, which I can't eat anyway because chocolate is bad for canines. She could have her party a week earlier or a week later. But don't get me started talking about how annoyed I was that I was now looking like the bad guy and Tom was suddenly Mister Perfect.

Linda was flying high. None of her "acts" had ever been invited to the White House. But when I told her why Tom was refusing to go and that Maggie would keep me company, she had a cow.

"What?!? Tom's giving up the White House for his kid's birthday? What a doofus! This is why I've always said you're not only the talent in this act, Larry, you're the brains too. Would you ever do something silly like that? Never! You don't even have to answer that."

The next day Linda bought one first-class airline ticket and a crate big enough for both Maggie and me. Linda thought the reason Maggie was coming along was because Cathy and Tom found a dog to keep me company. And Cathy and Tom thought Maggie was just a nice friend I'd met in the park one day. None of them knew the truth.

As we got ready to leave for the airport, I tried not to look back at the house, but just as I got in the car, I couldn't help but turn my head. I was sure I saw Cathy's face peeking at me from behind the curtains. I know she thinks I'm betraying Tom by going to Washington without him. And betraying her by not being there for her birthday. But the truth is I think they're both betraying me by not seeing that being invited to the White House was the most exciting thing that's ever happened in my life. And I just had to go!

"Now I know you're not the least bit nervous to perform without Tom, are you?" Maggie asked me as Linda supervised the limo driver, who was putting the suitcases in the trunk.

"You want those crates with the mutts in them in the trunk too?" I heard the driver say. And Linda actually thought about it!

"No shot," I hollered, and the limo driver's eyes got wide as he peered into my crate. Linda opened the crate and let us out.

"Oh yeah," the driver said. "It's that talking dog I saw on the news. How do you do that?" he asked Linda.

"Oh, I'm just that good," Linda said.

When we boarded the plane, Linda slid the crate under the seat in front of her. This time I didn't complain because I knew it would be nice being so close to Maggie for all those hours.

When we got to Washington, we asked the limo driver who picked us up at the airport to give us a tour of the city. Maggie and I stood on our hind legs at opposite open windows in the back, our faces blowing in the wind. It was cherry blossom time and the trees were a glorious pink, lining the streets to welcome us. I could see the Washington Monument reaching up to touch the beautiful blue sky, and then there was the famous Lincoln Memorial. Wow! It looked just the way it did on TV, only the statue of Abraham Lincoln was even bigger than I imagined.

I hollered out for the driver to stop the limo, and Maggie and I ran toward the steps leading up to the statue. I was sure President Lincoln's faithful dog Fido, the one I'd read about, would be shown sitting next to him, but when I got there . . . no Fido!

Maggie wasn't just beautiful. She was smart too. "Don't you know your canine history?" she asked. "Fido didn't go with the Lincoln family when they moved to Washington. President Lincoln was afraid Fido would miss Springfield, Illinois, too much."

"Now I remember," I said as we walked back to the waiting limo, where Linda sat talking on her cell phone.

"Yeah," I heard her say just before she saw us. "I'm taking my dog act to meet the Prez."

Her dog act?!? *I* was taking *her* to meet the President. And the only reason I brought her along at all was because I needed a human to turn doorknobs and push elevator buttons.

Back in the limo we navigated through the traffic and soon we saw the White House gleaming in the sun with its beautiful columns and the elegant lawn and the flag of our country waving in the breeze. I have to tell you it choked me up. Especially the lawn. I'll bet running on that lawn was the favorite thing to do for Barney and Buddy and Millie and all the other Presidential Dogs.

The minute we walked into the lobby of the Jefferson Hotel, some people recognized me. I could hear them whispering my name, but one old guy leaned over and said, "Cute little pup. A Terrier, right?" And he started rubbing my head way too hard for my taste. Linda nodded; she was busy checking us in. "Terriers are good ratters," he said, now rubbing even harder. "Stick their heads right down those rat holes and pull the rat out with their teeth."

"Not this Terrier," I announced and pulled away from him. The guy nearly fainted. I guess he was one of the few people who had never seen me on TV.

"The darn thing talked to me. I swear he just talked to me!" Maggie was laughing hysterically in the corner by a potted palm.

The White House! What can I say about the White House? We entered wearing our formal collars. A uniformed Marine guardsman walked us up the marble steps to where the state dinner was being held. Lots of ladies in long dresses and men in tuxes were everywhere, holding wineglasses, and a band of uniformed Marines was playing my song. I mean Tom's and my song, "I Want to Hold Your Paw."

Wow! I was rubbing ankles with the rich and famous. One of the Marines ushered us into a long line. And then in they came! The President and the First Lady.

My heart was pounding like crazy. And when I got to the front of the line and was standing near the President, he picked me up! He actually held me the way you sometimes see him holding his own dog on TV. He smiled at me and said, "If there is anyone on this planet I have been dying to meet, it's you." The President of the United States said that to me! I swear! That's exactly what he said.

"Well, likewise, I'm sure," I said. It was so astonishing seeing that famous face that would probably someday be on stamps looking right at me, Larry the Dog!

"All ready to do your show, little fella?" he asked.

"You betcha, Mister President," I said. Photos and flashes went off all around us. I turned and gave the press my toothiest grin.

"Well, let's go in to dinner," said the President.

In that big, beautiful, elegant formal dining room, Maggie and I sat right at the table. None of this eating on the floor stuff at the White House! The President sure knows how to treat his guests.

After dinner, when the Master of Ceremonies announced me, the First Lady leaned over and whispered, "Break a leg."

How can I describe the way it feels to be onstage at the White House looking out at a crowd of people in their very fanciest clothes? And right in the front row, holding hands with his wife, is the Leader of the Free World swaying side to side to my music? You gotta love it. Even if you're a Democrat and the President is a Republican, or the President is a Democrat and you're a Republican, or the President is a person and you're a dog or you're a person . . . Oh, never mind. You know what I mean.

I sang out and gave it everything I had. All of them were smiling and clapping along, and at the end of the number they all leapt to their feet cheering and applauding and yelling, "Bravo!"

I was blazing! Nothing could stop me now. I was a huge star and I knew it, and so did everyone else, including the President of the United States.

22
Cathy

Dad tried to act like he didn't feel bad about not being at the White House with Larry, but I know him too well. The morning of my party he blew up balloons and hung the piñata and grilled hot dogs and hamburgers, all the while smiling his biggest smile. But I knew he was thinking that he had missed the chance of his lifetime. And then I felt worse because I know he did it just for me.

I was on my way into the kitchen to thank him . . . or hug him . . . or just tell him that I love him. But I was stopped by an "oh, no" coming from the living room, so I ran in to see what happened.

My mother and Richard were staring at the television screen. "R-Richard wanted to check the basketball scores," my mother stammered. "And when he was flipping through the channels . . ." She couldn't find the words. She could only point in the direction of the television.

Larry was on TV being interviewed by that famous personality Larry Kane. Larry the Dog was sitting across from Larry Kane and he was wearing his sequined baseball cap turned backward, tilted just so. He didn't look like my sweet little Larry anymore.

". . . so the Vice President leaned over and whispered to me, 'Don't ever tell the President I told you this. But I came into the Oval Office last week and found him down on the floor. On his hands and knees. Talking to Alex, his Springer Spaniel. Saying, 'Come on, Alex . . . You can do it. If Larry can do it, you can too.' But the dog couldn't— or wouldn't—say a word. Not even to the most powerful man on earth," Larry the Dog said, then chuckled.

Larry Kane chuckled with him, then leaned forward with his chin on his fist and narrowed his eyes, like he was going to ask an important question.

"How'd you happen to get the same name as me?" Larry Kane asked with a sly smile.

"Did you ever think that *you're* the one who has the

same name as *me*?" Larry the Dog answered with a smug look on his furry white face.

"I think I had the name first." Larry Kane laughed. "I'm pretty sure I'm older than you."

"Maybe not in dog years . . ." Larry said.

They went to a commercial. I turned around to see that the whole living room had filled up with all the people from the party. My friends Lily and Abigail and their parents were laughing about everything Larry the Dog had just said. But Dad and Artie were standing at the back of the room saying nothing. And Mom and Richard and I were still standing in front of the television. None of us could move a muscle.

When the show started up again, Larry Kane pressed Larry the Dog further. "So tell me, Larry, what's up next in your career?"

"It's hard to say," Larry the Dog answered. "There were some pretty important people at the White House tonight and I've had some very big offers. My agent, Linda, has a lot of plans for me. Truthfully, she thinks it's time I go out on my own."

"See," Richard muttered. "I knew I never liked that dog."

"Richard, please . . ." my mother shushed him.

"Going out on your own?" Larry Kane asked, knowing he was leading Larry into trouble. "What about your partner, Tom?"

"Tom is great. And I owe a lot to him. But, let's face it, Linda says I'm where it's at."

Larry Kane pushed him. "Are you outgrowing him, Larry? Is his lack of drive holding you back? Do you think maybe the audience pays the high ticket price to see the genius of Larry the Dog and thinks of Tom as just the vehicle that got you where you needed to go?"

"Genius . . ." Larry repeated, taking the bait. "I guess you and my manager Linda are right. From now on, it'll be 'Larry the Dog.' In big bright lights. On my own. And the sky's the limit."

I turned around and looked at Dad. He was wearing a fake smile. "Well, that's it, everybody," he said. "Time for birthday cake!"

But when he leaned over to light the candles, Mom couldn't keep quiet. "That ungrateful little dog!" she said angrily.

"I hate to say I told you so," Richard said.

I tried to make excuses for Larry. "I think it's because

he's on television and the lights are probably making him a little crazy. He'll calm down once he's back here with us. He'll change his mind." But even I didn't believe what I was saying. I was sad because I knew that the dog on TV wasn't the little doggy I loved anymore. And from the hurt look on my dad's face, I could tell it was too late for Larry to fix things.

23
Larry

I was flying! I knew I did a great job on Larry Kane's show. I mean, even the camera crew was laughing at some of the funny things I said. Especially when I told Larry Kane that I might be older than he was in dog years. They loved that!

And what I said about me being the reason people loved the act, I didn't mean to hurt anybody. But, after all, it was true. Think about it. A guy playing the piano and singing. You've seen that a million times, right? But what you've never seen is a dog—a *Maltese*—who does what I do! Forget about it! I was the magic in the act. And that's what I said! That's *all* I said!

Back at the hotel suite Linda was in the bedroom packing up our stuff. Maggie hadn't said a word to me, but I figured she was just keeping quiet because Linda was there and she didn't want Linda to know she could talk.

"Well," I said to Maggie when I heard Linda busy on the phone in the other room. "Guess I'm a big hit around here! Larry Kane loved me! He even invited me to come back on the show." Maggie jumped on a chair so she could look out the window; her back was turned to me. "Didn't you think I was funny?" I asked.

She didn't answer for a long time. Then she turned to me. "You could have been a little more gracious about Tom," she said. "Not very cool to trash your human."

"Tom, Tom, Tom. I am so sick of always having to tiptoe around Tom," I barked. "He doesn't *own* me anymore! He's my *partner!* I am his equal. That's the problem with you dogs. You let people rule you and then they walk all over you."

"*You* dogs!" Maggie said, looking at me with a frosty glare. "You mean you're not a dog anymore? Well, that doesn't surprise me, Larry." And then she turned her back to me again.

Maggie didn't talk to me the whole way back to LA. In fact, she only spoke to me when we got to Los Angeles International Airport and she saw Linda was chatting with the limo driver as he put the bags in the trunk. And then it was only to remind me to tell the driver to drop her off.

"Drop Maggie at the bottom of Mandeville Canyon," I told the driver as we got onto the 405 Freeway. Linda had fallen asleep, so she never even saw Maggie jump out the door and hurry up the canyon to her human's house, or the sadness on my face as she left. Linda didn't open her eyes till we got to Tom's house.

"You gonna be okay, Lar?" she asked sleepily as I hopped out. All I wanted to do was go right in the doggy door and curl up in my bed.

"See ya, Linda," I said. I ran toward the house and hurled myself at the doggy door the way I always do, but—ouch!—this time I hit my head really hard.

"What the heck is this?" I said out loud and then looked carefully at the doggy door. It had been boarded up! There was something written on the boards. It was my name, Larry, with a big X over it!

The limo driver was just about to pull away when I ran toward the car, yelling, "Wait!" And he stopped.

"What is it?" Linda asked.

"They've locked me out!" I wailed.

"Really?" Linda asked. She got out of the limo and walked to the front door. Flapping in the breeze was a note that had been taped there.

*Postman, please discontinue delivering any mail
here for Larry the dog. He no longer lives here
and his forwarding address is unknown.*

"Whoa, I'll bet Tom saw you on Larry Kane and was pretty upset," Linda said. "Jeez, Lar, what are you going to do?"

"What am I going to do? Don't you mean, 'Poor Larry, my most successful client, please get back in the car and come to my house, where I will roll out the red carpet for you until you can find a place of your own'?"

Linda burst out laughing. "Don't be ridiculous," she said. "My building doesn't allow pets."

"Pets?" I shrieked at her. I was tired and furious at Tom and especially furious at Cathy, who must have been in on it. How could they do this to me? I mean, what did I do that was so terrible? Lots of acts break up. Lots of people go out on their own. And now Linda, my "loyal" agent, was turning on me too!

Well, I couldn't stand it, so I really let loose. "Pets? I am the greatest phenomenon in the world and you're putting me into the category of pets? You know what, Linda? I am going out first thing in the morning to find another agent to represent me, one who would never dream of living in a building where they're so narrow-minded they actually forbid dogs from the premises!"

"What? After all I've done for you?" Linda screamed. "You'd better not even dream about leaving me, Larry. I made 'Tom and Larry' the biggest act in the business, and I won't let you go. Ever! So don't get mouthy with me."

"Oh yeah?" I screamed right back. "Well, you'd better drop the name Tom from that sentence, because it looks as if he and I are through. So if you want to keep me, tonight you're going to break the rules of your building and have a visiting pet, and tomorrow you'll make two phone calls. One to the building manager to tell them I'm living in your place and the other one to Tom to tell him to find another agent. If he doesn't want me, it'll just be Larry, Larry, Larry, Larry, Larry. In films, on Broadway, my own TV series, maybe my own magazine, a few new albums, a music DVD. Got that?"

"Yeah, I got it," Linda said as she opened the door of the limo. I hopped in and the driver headed toward her apartment building, my new home. Neither of us spoke for the entire ride, but Linda did rub my head where I'd bumped it.

Unfortunately my head wasn't what hurt the most. What hurt the most was that deep inside I felt all alone in a way only Cathy could make better when she picked me up and hugged me and kissed me and told me how much she loved me. And now that I had been kicked out of the only real home I'd ever known and was going to live heaven knows where with someone who only hung out with me because it made her some money, I felt hurt all over.

Linda lived in the penthouse apartment in a building on Sunset Boulevard. As much as I hated being carried, I let her pick me up and walk me through the lobby. The doorman was dressed in a fancy uniform and he sneered when he saw her carrying me, but she slipped him a big wad of money and said, "Believe me, this is temporary. You know I'm not a dog person." That annoyed me, but I was too desperate to say anything.

"Killer apartment," I said to Linda as we walked into her place. There were big windows all around with views of the whole city, and plush velvety couches and chairs, and a giant round bed with a fake fur bedspread.

I jumped up on it and suddenly I heard her scream, "Off the bed. No dogs on my bed."

My mouth fell open in shock. "I beg your pardon!" I said. "If no dogs can be on the bed, where do you propose I sleep?" I asked.

"I'll make a box for you in the laundry room," she said.

I jumped off the bed and followed her. Sure enough she

went into the laundry room next to the washer and dryer with a big cardboard box and she started fluffing a towel she'd placed in it. Not even a soft and pretty towel—some old beach towel she didn't care about getting messed up.

"Okay, here's your bed," she said and then looked long at me. "Gosh, I'm so afraid you're going to shed all over everything and the maid was just here today."

"Uh, Maltese don't shed," I informed her.

She laughed a big red-faced laugh. "Oh sure," she said and then patted the towel. "Jump in here, boy."

"Linda, sweetie," I said to her, "I'll take the bed, you take the box." Then I walked to her room, slammed the door, jumped on the big, beautiful, soft, cushy bed and fell into a deep, miserable sleep.

24
Cathy

A long sad week went by after Dad locked Larry out of the house. Dad went back to playing the piano for other singers. In fact, he played on a few tracks again for Courtney Mason. He told me when he first walked in she slapped him on the back when she saw him and said, "Saw your dog on Larry Kane, dude! What a downer that must have been for you when he left. I guess you just can't trust anyone in this business."

It was finally the day of the school fair. I was selling tickets at the Dunk-A-Dad booth that I had been getting ready for weeks. It was going to be great. I really wanted to sell more tickets than Peter, who was in charge of the Knock Over the Stuffed Penguin booth. Mom was there too, running the bake sale. Whenever I walked past her, she slipped me one of my favorite cookies.

To make my booth the most successful, Dad agreed to be one of the dads who sat on the plank where everyone would try to dunk him in the water. Thanks to the fact that everybody knew him because of "Tom and Larry," lots of kids were standing in line to buy tickets before it was time for Dad to climb up the ladder to get in place.

As we made our way toward the booth, we heard a big cheer go up. Through the crowd, we saw my hand-painted sign on the front of the booth with its big multicolored letters that said DUNK-A-DAD. Then we saw a little white paw come up and we watched as it scratched out the word DAD and wrote in the word DOG.

It was Larry. I couldn't believe he showed up!

Mom walked up beside me. "He just got here a minute ago," she whispered to me. "He told me he thought if he showed up at a family event and tried to be a good sport, he might be welcomed back into the family."

I watched the crowd shout, "Lar-ry! Lar-ry!" as he made his way up the ladder and climbed out on the plank. Dad and Mom and I pushed our way up to the front of the group just in time to see Larry perch himself on the end of the wood, his "arms" crossed casually in front of him. He looked out at the crowd, his dog lips turned up in a smile.

"Whoa! Look! It's the dumb dog who sings on TV," sneered Derek. "Who wants to be the one to dunk him in the water first?"

"You do it," said one of the boys around him, egging him on. Derek was the pitcher on the softball team.

Larry sat back and flashed me a confident glance as Derek picked up the three rubber balls. The first ball plopped into the water without even hitting the platform.

"I must have been trying too hard," Derek said, winding up the second ball. With that one he managed to hit the bull's-eye target but not hard enough to even budge the plank.

Now he was determined. He was talking to himself, getting all psyched up. He rubbed the ball back and forth between his palms. He focused on the target, squinching his eyes real tight. And then he threw it as hard as he could.

We all watched the ball fly through the air. It looked like it would be long enough. It looked like it would be hard enough. But it was just a little too high.

Then Larry jumped up and caught the ball in his mouth. Just like he caught the Frisbee the ten zillion times I threw it to him.

A cheer went up from the crowd. Larry pranced around the plank and took a bow.

Then he took the ball out of his mouth, looked directly at me and said, "Hey, Cathy. That ought to show you how much everybody likes me. Even if you don't!"

I could feel my face getting redder and redder. I felt Dad tug at my arm and lead me away and I was glad to go. I didn't know what to say to Larry. And, by the look on his face, Larry didn't know what to say to me now either.

25
Larry

After the school fair, I knew I blew it. Cathy didn't understand that the reason I showed up there was so the family could see me take part in something important to her and her school. She was probably mad because I'm such a big show-off I couldn't help trying to be the center of attention again. When I got home, I was sadder than ever.

You'd think I'd feel better since we moved into a big new apartment. Linda hated sleeping on the living room sofa where she found herself after I told her to sleep in the box. And she was especially unhappy when I discovered that a few of her phony blonde strands of hair had come off on the pretty velvet sofa.

"Someone here is shedding," I teased, "but it isn't me!"

So the next day she signed a lease for a new apartment

across the hall, only this one had two huge bedrooms. I guess Linda was doing so well from me that she could afford it. And on moving day, when I saw her moving her wardrobe box toward the bedroom with the really great view, I said, "I'd like to look out over the city that worships me." She grudgingly moved her things into the smaller room. Hee-hee!

The new place was awesome. Lucky for me Maggie knew she had a job to do for dogdom, so she got over being mad at me. To keep me happy, Linda sent a car to pick her up every day. She'd come by to hang out and we'd have lunch and watch videos (my favorites were *Homeward Bound: The Incredible Journey* and *The Wizard of Oz,* although when Miss Gulch threatens Toto, I put my paws over my eyes). But late at night, after Maggie went home, I'd look out at the twinkling lights of LA from the twenty-fifth floor and think, It's lonely at the top.

Some nights, I would wake up from a bad dream and look around for Cathy. When I slept in her bed, she'd always comfort me when I'd wake up whimpering from one of those scary dreams dogs have (maybe about Miss Gulch).

"Maybe you should have a party," Maggie said to me on one of her visits. "It might cheer you up."

"But I have nobody to invite," I told her. "Cathy and Tom won't come, and the dogs are all angry at me, so who would be here?"

"Maybe some of the rock stars you've met in your travels?" she tried. So we bought invitations. While I typed the names of the guests on my computer, Maggie looked over my shoulder, or where my shoulder would be if dogs had shoulders.

"Maybe if you invited Tom and Cathy, it would be a good way to make up?" Maggie suggested.

But I shook my head sadly. "It won't work," I told her. "I've messed up too badly."

The day of the party, Linda drove Maggie and me to a spa so we would look great that evening. The groomer was a beautiful girl with hair the color of Cathy's, but her eyes were not as blue as Cathy's, and her smile was not as pretty as Cathy's. She gave me a great haircut while I sat and missed Cathy.

Afterward, on Rodeo Drive, Maggie and I bought two matching spiked leather collars. As I looked into the mirror at the two of us when we walked into the lobby of the building, I saw the beautiful Maggie walking with a dog who looked very fancy but very unhappy.

Actually the way my white hair was flying wildly I looked liked Albert Einstein. Cathy and I used to have that as a joke. She would fluff the fur on my head till it looked very wild and then say, "Hiya, Mr. Einstein!" It always made us both laugh.

With all the rock stars having a great time at the party, my apartment building shook like there was a huge earthquake that night. Linda mingled with everyone and chatted away as if they'd come to see her. The music was loud and everyone danced and sang along. The conversation was all about me, the cake was iced with a white coconut version of me, the songs playing on my music system were my songs. So why wasn't I out there dancing happily with the others?

"Wicked haircut there, Lar. You are so the bomb!" Courtney Mason said.

"Kind of like Albert Einstein," I said and laughed. But she had already walked away.

I wanted to scream out, "Go home, all of you." But mostly I wanted to go home myself.

"We need more ginger ale," I heard someone say and I headed toward the kitchen to see if we had any left. Linda was in there putting some sandwiches on a tray to take out to the guests when she saw my face.

"Boy, do you look down in the dumps, Lar," she said,

picking up a handful of napkins that had my picture on them. "Isn't this a great day for you, all these people showing up at your party?"

"I guess," I told her. "But I think I'd give it all up for a hug from Cathy."

Linda's phone rang and she grabbed it. I walked out into the living room to watch everyone have a great time. In a minute Linda rushed into the room excitedly. Then she raised a glass and tapped on it with a spoon to get everyone's attention.

"I just wanted to welcome you all to our party and to announce that I just got word that Larry's been invited to sing 'The Star-Spangled Banner' at the Dodgers' opening game next week."

Cheers and "Wow!" and "Cool" went up from the crowd.

"I'm so proud of you," Maggie whispered, beaming.

"Do you think it will get Tom and Cathy to like me again?" I asked.

"I don't know," Maggie said softly. "I hope so."

26
Cathy

It had been two months since Dad and Larry split up and to me every day seemed like a year. To make a bad time even worse, today I had to go shopping with Mom for the dress she wanted me to wear in her wedding.

I looked at myself in the mirror wearing a fabulous lavender silk dress, which might have looked better on me if only I could have smiled.

"Cathy, honey," she said. "Please tell me what's going on with you. You know there isn't anything you can't say to me."

Tears rushed into my eyes. "Everything's wrong. Larry's gone and I miss him. And I want you to still be married to Dad, not to Richard," I blurted out.

"Aww, honey," she said, hugging me. "I know why you feel that way, but Richard cares about you and he's even promised to try really hard to like dogs."

"Sure, Mom," I said as a salty tear fell into my mouth. "Except that I don't have a dog anymore."

"Well, I have good news," she said. "Richard suggested when we finish here that you and I go over to the SPCA and see if there's another dog you can fall in love with. And Richard will be extra nice to him. I promise."

"Another dog?" I asked, surprised. "How could I get another dog? It would be like I went away to camp and you brought home another kid to live in my room. I could never do that to Larry."

"You're not doing anything to Larry, sweetie," she said. "Larry has a different life now. And if you love him as much as I know you do, you'll understand that it makes him happy to sing and dance and be a big star."

"Happier than it made him to be my dog?" I asked.

"Just because it isn't a life that you would choose or your dad would choose, it *is* what Larry chose. And everybody gets to choose for himself. So let's go see if we can find a dog that will want to just be a doggy kind of dog," Mom said, as she slung an arm around my shoulder and led me toward the door.

I let Mom drag me to the pound even though my heart wasn't in it.

"What about this one?" Mom asked as we went down the row of cages.

I kept shaking my head no to all of them. I was looking for a Maltese like Larry. "He's not small enough." "He's not fluffy enough." "He's not . . ."

"Honey," Mom said, "you shouldn't try to find one exactly like Larry. Let's try to get a completely different type of dog. It'll be too hard on the dog and too hard on you if you try to get someone just like Larry."

I knew she was right. One of my favorites was a cute little black-and-white Pug, but he seemed more interested in taking his nap than in sniffing at my hand. Then I went down the line and there was a Jack Russell Terrier who was jumping up and down in the cage. But I thought he might do that all night and I'd never get to sleep.

And then I saw an Old English Sheepdog. The person in charge told me he was already eight years old and no one else seemed to want a dog that big and furry and old.

The Sheepdog came over to me and looked straight into my eyes and I could swear he winked at me. I laughed out loud and both my mother and the SPCA person thought I was a little weird because they didn't see anything funny. But I turned to Mom and said, "Let's take him."

"Whoa, honey! Are you sure?" Mom said, surprised. "He's awfully big."

"I'm positive. He's friendly and cuddly and he's meant to be my new dog. I can just tell."

"Okay," she told the SPCA man, looking at the name written on the card on his cage. "I guess we'll take Elliot."

"Elliot," I said. "I like that name."

While Mom went inside to fill out all the papers with the SPCA man, Elliot trotted out behind me with a little bounce in his walk that I'd never seen on such a big furry creature. Then he stopped and stretched out his body the way dogs do. First his front two "arms" (which is what I call them even though the vet laughs at me) and then he rolled out his back and then he stretched out his back legs one at a time. Boy, I guess he was really glad to be out of that cage!

I took Elliot for a walk around the property and he

slurped my hand as I held on to his leash as if he was saying, "thank you." Then when we stopped under a big elm tree, I felt a big gentle paw rest on my shoulder. I turned around to see Elliot leaning toward my ear.

"Larry's in a lot of trouble," he said.

27
Larry

A cold wind cut through my fur as I walked out of Linda's building and looked for my driver. He opened the back door of the big long stretch limo the record company was now sending for me wherever I went. I jumped into the car and tried to relax as it went weaving along Sunset Boulevard. I put my paw on the button for the power window. I needed to let the fresh air blow through my fur. I needed to clear my head.

When we stopped at a light, I watched a woman walking across Sunset Boulevard with a white Bichon Frise under her arm. She scratched its ear while they walked and the dog turned his head and licked her hand.

And as we passed Roxbury Park, a place where I used to romp and play with Cathy, I saw a man in shorts running next to his beautiful black Lab, and I thought how alone I was without my humans to be there with me. I wondered if they ever looked around and thought life wasn't as much fun without me. Or if they had already forgotten about me.

Maybe Tom and Cathy would even be at today's Dodgers game and they would realize how much they missed me too. At least that's what I hoped. After all, the fact that I was going to sing the National Anthem at the opening game of the season had been advertised in the newspaper and on TV for days.

Everyone said it was "A big deal for anyone but especially for a dog." I didn't like them putting it that way. It was an honor, I'll admit. But I've already proven what a star I am. So why shouldn't they give it to me?

When I got to Dodger Stadium, more than fifty thousand people had filled the stands. The big Jumbotron in center field showed me waiting with Linda in the box behind home plate and everyone in the stadium started chanting, "Lar-ry! Lar-ry! Lar-ry!"

At exactly two o'clock, the announcer called the name of each of the players from the visiting team, the New York Mets. One by one the players took the field to polite applause and took their place along the third base line. When the announcer introduced the Dodgers, the crowd went wild as they lined up along the first-base line.

And then it was time for me. The crowd got quiet. The announcer's voice boomed through the stadium. "Ladies and gentlemen . . . To sing the National Anthem today, one of our biggest new stars . . . Lar-ry . . . the . . . Dog!"

The crowd yelled and cheered as I trotted out to home plate wearing a little Dodger cap that the team had made especially for me. I tried to appear nonchalant but I must admit it was pretty exciting. After all, I was a big Dodgers fan (even though I had to watch them play every season up till now in silence).

The first bars of the music blared through the sound system. Everyone in the stadium stood and put their hands over their hearts. I opened my mouth to sing:

Oh, say can you see . . .

Uh-oh. That didn't sound right. Maybe it was the echo in here.

By the dawn's early light . . .

Nothing came out but a hoarse-sounding croak. I looked around nervously. I was sure everyone was staring at me with funny expressions on their faces.

What so proudly we hail . . .

I could feel my throat getting tighter and tighter.

The crowd had stopped singing along and was listening to me make some hoarse noises that I prayed sounded even a little like the National Anthem. It took forever before I got to the words *"O'er the land of the free . . . and the home of the brave."*

The umpire finally called, "Play ball!" and as the teams went into their dugouts, I ran off the field so quickly you would have thought a Rottweiler was chasing me.

Linda was waiting at the edge of the field and she scooped me up and got me out of there as fast as she could. "This is all I need," she said. "You with no voice! Do you know how many tickets we've sold for your concert this weekend? You should have heard how croaky and awful you sounded . . . and that's when I could hear you making any sound at all!" She practically threw me into her car, and we headed straight for the vet's office.

I hated going to the vet. Even though Dr. Blakemore was gentle and sweet, she still was the one who had to give me all those ouchy vaccinations, and undignified checkups.

Linda told her what had happened at Dodger Stadium. "Thousands of people are coming to hear him Saturday night at the Hollywood Bowl," Linda shrieked into the doctor's face. "Fix him!"

"I think it's best that Larry and I are alone," the doctor said. For that I could have slurped her pretty face.

When Linda huffed out of the room, slamming the door

behind her, Dr. Blakemore turned her gaze on me. "Can you talk?" she asked.

I shook my head.

"Let's have a look at you then," she said. I opened my mouth. She looked at my throat for a long time and then felt my glands. When she finished, she sat in a chair next to the examining table. "Larry, I've been expecting this visit from you for a while. In fact, I'm surprised it's taken this long for you to come in here. Your throat is fine. Your physical health seems perfect. I'm afraid, however, that something is really wrong with the way you're living your life.

"I think you lost your voice because you feel bad about yourself. I can spray your throat so you can sing this weekend. But you have to promise me that when the concert is over, you'll take a close look at what you're doing."

I opened my mouth and she sprayed my throat. As she left the examination room, I was able to say, "Thank you, Doctor." But I knew I was far from cured.

28
Cathy

Elliot and I instantly became good friends. "Look," he said to me that first night when we were sitting in my room, "I know I shouldn't be talking to you and telling you our secrets. But the other dogs say you can be trusted, after the way you kept Larry's secret up until he went nuts at Clementine Flowers' concert and told the whole world."

"Is that why he's in trouble?" I asked.

"Darned right. He could have really screwed things up for all of us dogs just by opening his big mouth. And there are dogs that have their fur in a twist about it. Some pretty tough breeds that I wouldn't want to meet up with on a dark dog run."

"What's going to happen to him, Elliot? What can we do to help him?"

"Nothing, really," Elliot answered. "The cat's already out of the bag, as they say. Let's just hope he handles himself right from now on. And makes it look as if he's the only talking dog on earth. Then they'll let it die down. Otherwise . . ." And he shook his head ominously.

I tried to go to sleep, but I was really scared. We all knew what a quick temper Larry had. Any little thing could set him off, and when it did, he could do crazy things without thinking.

But Larry's life was his own now, and my life was going to be about me and Elliot. The next day I decided to take Elliot to Roxbury Park. But as we were walking there, along the sidewalk in the middle of town, we saw a big crowd in front of a restaurant blocking the whole street. Elliot and I tried to scoot along the curb to get past them, but the closer I got to them, the more I realized they weren't just people waiting for a table. This was a big group standing around watching as a camera crew set up tripods. Then they moved those big white reflectors so the sun didn't shine in the eyes of the person they were shooting. All of a sudden I heard a familiar voice holler:

"Yo, don't you even say hello anymore?"

I whipped around just in time to see Larry strolling over to me.

"What's going on, Larry?" I forced myself to smile at him.

"They're taking my picture. I'm going to be on the cover of *Rolling Stone*."

"How nice," I said, feeling happy for him in spite of everything. "I'm glad to see you have the life you wanted."

"Not really," Larry said. "I wanted this, but I wanted to be your dog too."

"Well, you know what Mick Jagger says . . ." Then I started to sing. "*You can't always get–*"

"*–what you want,*" Larry finished the line for me. "Yeah, yeah, I know. *But if you try sometimes . . .*"

"And that's what you got, Larry. Just *what you need.* I'm happy for you. I really am."

"You know I have a big concert coming up this Saturday. At the Hollywood Bowl. It's all sold out. But I can always leave tickets for you," he said hopefully. "I'd love for you to come, Cathy."

"My dad and I have plans. You remember . . . it's our regular night out. The kind our family used to have."

Then I thought I heard a little catch in his voice when he said, "Maybe you could both come?"

"Larry, don't you get it?" I tried to say it as kindly as I could. "My dad doesn't want to see you."

Larry stiffened his lower black lip and said, "He hurt me as much as I hurt him. He locked me out. Boarded up the dog door. Told me I didn't live there anymore."

"What did you expect would happen after what you said on *The Larry Kane Show*? That things would just go back to normal? That you'd live in our house after you embarrassed my father on national television?"

Before Larry could answer, the photographer called him. "Let's go, Larry. Before we lose the light."

Larry turned to look at the photographer and when he turned back, he saw that Elliot had walked up beside me. "Who's the big lug?" he said.

"This is Elliot. He's my dog."

He looked Elliot up and down. "A big galumphy Sheepdog? This is who you got to replace me?"

"You bet," I answered.

And then, for the first time since he started talking, Larry had nothing to say.

29
Larry

My big show was that night. Maggie and I took a long walk so I could get the kinks out of my legs. I didn't want to admit I was nervous since I'd been performing for big crowds for a while now, but this was different. It was going to be the first time I sang in concert in my hometown since Tom and I split up. Besides, after losing my voice at Dodger Stadium the other day, I feared looking foolish in front of a lot of people again.

We went to the park around the corner from Linda's apartment and ran around, chasing each other and behaving like ordinary dogs. For just a little while I wanted to be like an ordinary dog and forget everything else. A dog that didn't have to worry about human problems but could just play all day and be loved.

Afterward, Maggie and I stretched out on the grass to

rest and let the sunlight shine down on us. It felt so warm and cozy that we both fell asleep.

I woke up when I heard a woman call to her Beagle. "Let's go, Bowser. Everyone will be waiting for us for dinner."

Ohmigosh! I jumped up, waking Maggie. "C'mon, c'mon," I whispered in her ear so no one else could hear us talking. "We overslept. I'm going to be late. Let's go!"

Maggie and I rushed out of the park and back toward Linda's apartment building. When I noticed an alleyway that would be a shortcut home, I nudged Maggie. "Let's go this way. It'll take us to the back driveway."

We were deep into the alley when three fierce-looking dogs stepped out from behind a Dumpster. I looked into the faces of a German Shepherd and a Great Dane who were standing next to an angry little Papillon. It was the Papillion who spoke.

"Hold it right there, pal," he said in a voice that sent chills up my spine. "This is a warning," the Papillon went on. "Maggie may think she can keep you from talking, but just remember—we're watching you too. You'd better not dream of ratting on us, Mr. Larry the Star. Or you're gonna be Larry Burgers. You got me?"

"Boys, please," I said, flashing them my biggest smile to

try to cover the fact that I was shaking. "I'm not going to spill the beans. You have to believe me."

But they didn't. And in one quick move the German Shepherd backed me up against the wall.

"You rat us out and you'll regret it," the Great Dane announced.

Maggie stepped between me and the Shepherd. "Easy, guys. Back off," she cooed. "Larry is our friend. He said he wouldn't talk about us and he hasn't."

"Only because you're around to keep his muzzle on," sneered the Papillon. "Larry is not to be trusted. He's already proven that to all of dogdom."

At that moment a back door opened and a man came outside lugging a big trash bag. As he approached the nearby Dumpster, all three dogs looked over their shoulders at him and ran off in three different directions.

I tried not to let Maggie see how rattled those dogs made me. "Rat them out? Why would I do that?" I fumed.

"Calm down," Maggie soothed.

"Well, I don't like being threatened," I huffed.

"They know you, Larry. They know you fly off the handle and act without thinking. You've done it before. Look at the way you let Cathy and Tom know you could talk in the first place. To say nothing of what you did when you ran out onstage and let the whole world know you could sing."

"Look, I just wanted some credit for writing that song too. I had to be smuggled inside Cathy's backpack that night. I was treated like I was invisible! Do you know how that made me feel?"

"That's the problem with you, Larry. It's always about you. You, you, you." Maggie was getting hot under her plaid collar. And then she said the words I dreaded. "You know, Larry, I'm going to call Solomon the Shar-Pei and tell him I don't want this job anymore. Ever since you trashed your human on television I thought about leaving you, only I was too concerned for the dog world to do it. But I can see more and more that your ego is too big. Nothing and no one can stop you from doing what you want. And you're not worth my time anymore."

"Wait, Maggie," I heard myself crying out. But she just kept walking away with her tail in the air. She never even looked back at me.

I went home and tried to block out how bad I felt. But I kept seeing Maggie's face as she was telling me off. And then I saw Cathy's face in my mind and, yes, even Tom's face. And no matter how much I tried to distract myself by spraying my throat and gargling to make sure I could go out there and wow everyone with my new act and the great new songs I had written, I felt worse than I had in years. And in dog years you multiply that by seven.

My thoughts were interrupted by Linda, who called out from the living room, "Wait until you see this. You aren't going to believe it!"

I ambled into the living room, jumped up onto the window seat and looked down into the courtyard in front of the building. It was a sea of photographers waiting to see me on my way to the Hollywood Bowl.

"Look at them down there. All waiting for you!" Linda jumped up and down. "My star client. Larry the Dog! Let's go down there and give them a thrill as we head for the car!" she said, giddy with excitement.

"I'm ready," I told her and the two of us headed toward the elevator. I tried to push my sadness out of my mind to get ready to face my public. On the elevator my heart started to pound. I couldn't wait to get out there and give them my interview. To tell them it was going to be the best show anyone had ever seen. Maybe that would make me feel better. Get me "up" for the show, as they say.

The elevator doors opened. Someone yelled, "It's him," and the reporters rushed into the lobby. That same doorman who once sneered at me lifted me onto the reception desk so everyone could see me as I flashed them my biggest and best Larry smile.

They shouted hundreds of questions all at once about the concert and my future plans. I tossed out the answers and tried to hear the next questions coming at me, as I tried to stay one step ahead of them. I was fielding each question like the star I had become, getting laughs and cheers for my clever and witty replies.

So it took me by surprise . . . threw me off guard . . . when one of them shouted out, "What do the other dogs think about you, Larry?"

"You mean there *are* other dogs?" I joked. That got a big laugh.

"Well, sometimes," the reporter said, "it doesn't seem like it. Since none of them can talk, and you talk a blue streak."

"That's why Larry the Dog is such a big star," Linda interrupted.

The reporter ignored her and pressed his microphone closer to me.

"Why do you think that is?" he asked, his eyes narrowing.

"Beats me." I tried to shrug it off.

"Do you think you're smarter than other dogs?"

My back stiffened because he was starting to annoy me. Then he pushed me too far.

"Or are other dogs just stupid?" he continued rudely.

That was it for me. That insult was more than I could bear. So once again, old hothead me lost my cool big-time.

"Stupid! You think dogs are stupid?" I said, in a voice filled with rage. "Dear boy, if you think that, then you are the one who is an American Kennel Club–certified moron! Dogs are so far from stupid they manage to have man supporting them, waiting on them hand and foot, giving them food, shelter, and adoration just for being their silent and what they are convinced is their obedient best friend."

"Then why is it they can't even manage to utter one little word?" that same reporter pressed.

"Ha! The truth is that all dogs *can* talk and have plenty of opinions and ideas but are so much smarter then men and women that they *refuse* to talk, so they can continue to be pampered by stupid humans like you!"

There was a long silence. All the reporters just stood there staring at me in shock. Then, when what I said hit home, the place went wild. Everyone started screaming at once.

"They can talk? My Yorkie can talk?"

"You mean all dogs? Are you sure?"

"All these years they've heard my secrets and now you're saying they can talk about them? Oh no!"

Linda and I just barely made it into our waiting limo, and the driver had to navigate carefully through the people. A few reporters jumped on the hood of the car, pounding on the window.

Finally the limo was in the clear. We slowly headed up Highland Avenue toward the Hollywood Bowl. I felt weak and afraid.

"Driver," I said, "turn the radio to 900 on the dial."

"There's no station there, sir," the driver answered.

"Do it," I barked.

The driver turned the limo radio dial to 900. KNIN. And I could hear what neither he nor Linda could. They were playing and replaying sound bites from my interview. "They *refuse* to talk, so they can continue to be pampered by stupid humans like you!" And then the host of the show was shouting that I'd gone too far. "It's time to rise up! To stop him!" he said.

Next a Collie he was interviewing spoke up. "Maybe some of my Pit Bull friends should pay Larry a visit."

"No," the host barked. "That's what people would do. We're a higher form of life."

The Collie wasn't ready to give up. "Maybe. But Larry certainly doesn't act like it."

"Oh, God. What have I done?" I said out loud.

"Oh, honey, relax. All you did was stir up a lot of publicity for the show. Not that you needed it. I mean we're already sold out."

"Yes," I said. "Sold out. That's what I've done. I've sold out."

"Lighten up, fur face," she said. "Not a big deal. The dogs will be better off. Now pull yourself together and get ready to knock them all dead!"

30
Cathy

Whenever Dad and I go to the movies, we buy the biggest box of popcorn they have and choose some stupid comedy that cracks us up and makes us forget that maybe we weren't feeling so great when we came in. Today he picked me up at Mom's house. As I ran downstairs, I heard my mom and Richard talking in the living room, but when I got there they both stopped talking.

"I think Dad just drove up," I said. They were too distracted to say anything but "Great." Because Dad was honking the horn, I waved good-bye and shouted, "I won't be late," as I ran out the door.

As we drove along Hollywood Boulevard, Dad was busy trying not to notice what was hard to miss—that every billboard had a picture of Larry. Even on the car radio there were blasting ads for Larry's hot concert that night at the Hollywood Bowl.

We were on our way to the theaters at Hollywood Boulevard and Highland Avenue, but there was so much traffic we were afraid we'd be late and miss the beginning of the movie. Dad finally found a parking lot that was a block away from the movie theater. We hopped out of the car and suddenly I stopped talking and grabbed Dad's arm because what I saw was the scariest thing I'd ever seen in my life.

"Look!" I hollered. It was a stampede of dogs, thousands of dogs, heading up Highland Avenue, running north in the direction of the Hollywood Bowl, and they all had angry, fierce expressions on their faces. Dad and I moved against a building to avoid being crushed. Something terrible must have happened.

After the onslaught of dogs passed, we saw a bunch of people in a restaurant all gathered around a television set. They seemed to be watching a newscast, so Dad and I opened the door and joined them.

"In a startling revelation just moments ago from popular entertainer Larry the Dog, the world found out what had to be the best-kept secret for thousands and thousands of years, as old as mankind. On his way to perform in his solo concert at the Hollywood Bowl, Larry the Dog told reporters a bit of jaw-dropping information. When asked why other dogs besides himself didn't speak, and could the reason be that other dogs were simply too stupid, the explosive Larry turned with anger on a reporter."

I looked at my Dad in horror as I saw Larry come on the TV screen and say, "The truth is that all dogs *can* talk!"

Everyone in the restaurant was shocked and buzzing about it to one another. One woman even started to cry. "All these years and my poor Mimi never told me the truth," she said and pulled out a handkerchief.

On TV they had now turned the camera on the reporters who were going wild. They even showed the reporters jumping on Larry's limo and pounding on the hood. I felt the crowd of people around me slowly getting smaller as people walked out of the restaurant in a daze. I heard one lady say, "I'm going home to have a serious conversation with Spot." I looked over at Dad, who was standing there with a determined look.

"He's in trouble and he needs us, honey. We're still his family," he said. "You saw those dogs running up the street. They're going after him. We'd better get over to the Bowl as fast as we can to save Larry!"

Dad and I ran for his truck. He peeled out and drove as fast as he could toward the Hollywood Bowl, but the traffic was bumper-to-bumper—and it was made worse by the crowd of dogs running on the freeway between the stopped cars. Dad pulled the truck off at the Barham Boulevard exit and we parked. We jumped out and ran the rest of the way, passing more and more dogs headed the same way we were. The show was scheduled to start in half an hour. We had to get to Larry as quickly as we could.

"No matter what he's done, we still love him, don't we?" Dad said as we passed the lines of cars waiting to enter the parking lot at the Bowl.

"Absolutely!" I agreed as we rushed up the hill and a lady ticket-taker stopped us.

"You got a ticket?" she said.

"I'm Tom," Dad said to her.

"You're who?" she asked as a big bunch of dogs thundered past us. None of them had tickets but she didn't stop them.

"Of 'Tom and Larry,' " Dad said. "I used to be in the act with him. I have to get to him, please. Those dogs look as if they want to hurt him."

"Oh, yeah," the lady said, looking at Dad thoughtfully. "I remember when Larry had a human for a partner. And now I remember it was kind of a dull-looking guy like you."

"Thanks a lot," Dad said.

"Tom," she said, "I really shouldn't let you in without a ticket. But somebody's got to bring that dog to his senses, and you're probably the one to do it."

Then she turned to the next group of people, who handed her their tickets as Dad and I rushed toward the dressing rooms.

31
Larry

I had a stomachache and a headache, but mostly it was my poor heart that was aching. I looked out the window of the big fancy trailer that was set up for my dressing room. Up on the hill I could see a herd of dogs gathered together and staring down at my trailer. And I knew it was not because they were my fan club.

"Jeez," Linda said. "Those dogs look a little annoyed, Lar." If that wasn't the understatement of the year. "I hope none of the audience is put off, seeing all those dogs around. I'd better get over to the box office and see how we're doing."

With that she started to leave the trailer. Through the open door I suddenly caught a glimpse of Maggie pushing her tiny, delicate, beautiful way through the crowd. She was so small she managed to edge past Linda, who didn't even notice her.

I opened the door just far enough for Maggie to squeeze in through the crowd. She looked at me for a long time.

"Can you ever forgive me?" I asked.

"It isn't me forgiving you that matters, Larry. You need to beg forgiveness from Tom and Cathy. And you need to beg the forgiveness of all of dogdom for doing the most unforgivable thing of all: behaving like a human and giving up your dogness."

She was right, she was so right. I just didn't know what to do or how to fix it.

Suddenly there was another knock on the door. I was sure it was the stage manager telling me I had to go on. I never wanted to sing or dance again.

"Yes?" I said sadly.

"It's Cathy and Tom," I heard Cathy's voice say.

My heart danced in my chest. "My Cathy and Tom?" I asked stupidly as I opened the door.

The two of them looked exhausted. As if they'd been running for miles to get to me.

"My doggeee," Cathy said, and she rushed to hug me. We both cried as we hugged.

"I'm so sorry," I said, and then Tom joined in the hug.

"We still love you, Larry," Tom said. "We always will."

"I was the un-dog," I said. "A dog's best quality is his loyalty and I stopped being loyal. But I want to change that. I want to come home if you'll have me. I want to be your dog again. I want to make this nightmare go away."

"I'm afraid it's too late for that," Tom said, and we all peeked out the window together, where the crowd of dogs at the top of the hill was larger than before.

32
Cathy

I looked at the dogs and I looked at Larry and I knew he was afraid.

"We have to go up there, Larry," Maggie said. "So you can apologize."

"She can talk too?" Dad said.

"They all can," I admitted. He was surprised I knew that.

"And they'll never forgive me for telling the world," Larry said.

"Try them," I encouraged him. "Dogs are always loyal, so I'll bet they'll be loyal to you."

Larry looked around at Dad and Maggie and me. "If you three believe in me, maybe I can do it."

"We do."

When Larry heard that, he opened the door to the

trailer and led Maggie, Dad and me up the hill. Down below we could see the fans filing into the Hollywood Bowl. But the most important performance of Larry's life was about to happen before he even set foot on that stage.

Slowly we trudged up the hill but halfway there Larry stopped in his tracks, unable to go on. "I can't do this!" he said.

"If you tell them the truth, they'll understand," Dad said, encouraging him.

I picked Larry up in my arms and held him close. "We're your family and we'll be right here. Now walk up there and do what you have to do."

Larry licked my face like he used to in the old days and said, "I'm ready for them."

But when we got to the top of the hill and Larry started toward the crowd of dogs, Dad hollered out, "Good luck, Larry!" Well, that did it.

"Larry? Larry? Did someone say Larry?" The dogs all heard what Dad said and turned to see Larry climbing onto a nearby rock.

"Boo, it's him! There he is! The traitor! The big mouth! The turncoat!"

I held my hands up in a gesture of silence and called

out to them, "Wait! Stop! He's my dog and I forgive him. My dad forgives him. Can't you try to forgive him too?"

With his tail between his legs in a posture of submission, Larry looked around at their faces. "My friends . . ." he began.

"Boo-o-o, we're not your friends. Not anymore. You sold us down the river for a sequined hat! Boo-o-o!"

"Stop," Solomon the Shar-Pei cried out. "Act like dogs. Dogs don't hold grudges, dogs don't seek revenge! Let Larry speak." Finally they fell silent.

"My fellow dogs, I lost my head and I lost my dogness, and I'm so sorry. I know I could say that others pushed me into a corner and I just snapped, which is partly true, but I know that would really be just an excuse. As much as I wanted what was best for dogdom, I gave you away because of my foolish temper. I need you to know now that I really didn't mean to hurt any of you. And as much as I hurt you and hurt my humans, the one I hurt the most by everything I did was myself. That's why I humbly and with love in my heart beg you to forgive me."

Larry looked around for their reaction, but the dogs

looked at him, unimpressed. He kept on, trying to convince them.

"I know dogs have had a wonderful silent arrangement with mankind for all these years, and it has worked well for both dogs and their owners. Because something magical goes on between people and dogs that has nothing to do with words. The way we wag a tail, the way we run in circles at the feet of someone we love, the way we nuzzle our faces into their hands to say we need a pat. Those gestures say it all. Much more than any words ever could. One of the many things I've learned is that words are not as important as feelings. And when it comes to feelings, I'll take the feelings of dogs over the feelings of humans any day."

By now Larry had tears in his eyes.

"I want to be a real dog again. Man's best friend. Dogs don't lie, dogs don't cheat, dogs say more to their owners through their eyes than any word in any language could ever convey. Dogs are real; we don't care how we look or what we're wearing or what anyone thinks of us when we act silly—which we love to do—and when we act serious—which we sometimes do when we have to be responsible. We don't care who's rich and who's poor, we just want to love and be loved in return, and everything else is unimportant."

"Then why did you do what you did?" a Wirehaired Terrier called out to him.

"Because I let my dognity fall away, and tried to be human," Larry answered. "And I did it in the worst way— by taking on all of the most negative qualities any human can have. And for what? It wasn't worth it, and I want to come back. I want all of you to take me back as a full-fledged dog again."

"No chance," a Lhasa Apso exclaimed. "Unless you make everything right again."

"I'll try," Larry said, "because all I want in life is to come back to my family and be Cathy's sweet little pup and Tom's best friend and Elliot's brother. So if you'll allow me, I'm going to go out onstage now, and perform especially for all of you. And while I'm there and have the world's attention, I'll try to repair the damage. But I don't want to go out there alone. I want to go with my best friend beside me, singing along in very close harmony. My partner and human and friend, Tom." He turned to my dad. "Will you come out onstage and perform with me?"

It took Dad a minute while he absorbed what Larry

asked. Then he smiled a very big smile and said, "You bet."

When Dad and Larry and I got down the hill and headed into the backstage area to get ready to do the show, I saw my mom waiting there for us. I was surprised but very happy to see her. I rushed to her to give her a big hug.

"Where's Richard?" I asked her.

"He's gone," Mom said. "We broke up. It was the dog thing most of all." From the corner of my eye I could see Dad breathe a huge sigh of relief as Mom and I went to our seats in the front row.

It was the rocking and rollingest show in the history of rock and roll. Larry and Dad sang every song they could think of. They danced and leapt all around the stage and there were fireworks in the sky; the kind the Hollywood Bowl always sets off on the Fourth of July. And the people in the audience were dancing holding their dogs in their arms and the dogs and the people were full of smiles. A roar went up from the crowd when Dad and Larry finished their last song, and when they made their exit the audience wouldn't stop clapping until they came on to do an encore, and when the audience saw they were back they cheered and shouted,

"Tom, Larry, Tom, Larry," until Dad put his hand up to get them to stop and then Larry walked to the microphone.

"Friends, I said something to the news media today that was misunderstood and misinterpreted. Here is what I really meant. I said that all dogs can speak, and all of you who live with dogs know that dogs do speak! But not with words like me. Your dogs speak in their own way, which is from their wonderful hearts to the hearts of their owners.

"Every time they lick your hand, it's a thank-you; every time they snuggle up next to you, it's an I love you; every time they rush to the door barking when you get home, it's a thank heaven you're back. So doesn't that mean more than words, and doesn't that say everything dogs need to tell their humans? And aren't you glad they aren't chattering away needlessly the way some people do? I was one of those chatterers and I plan to go back to being the dog of Tom and Cathy from now on."

The audience cheered, and Larry and Dad rolled into the last verse of "Every Dog Gets His Day." I knew that this day belonged to Larry as all the dogs who had been there watching hurried to the stage to stand beside him while he and Dad sang. And when they got to the "arf, arf, arf, arf" part, even the dogs joined in.

When they finished, I couldn't wait to take my dog Larry home with Dad and me. As we headed for Dad's truck, I heard the announcer say over the PA system, "Ladies and gentlemen, Larry has left the building."